# "You never married?" Nick asked.

Julie's gaze dropped to her hands. She fiddled with the pen. "No. Never found the right guy."

He'd struck a nerve. Which made him more curious and stirred an ache in his chest he couldn't explain. Had someone hurt her? "I remember in high school you didn't date."

He'd chickened out and hadn't asked her to homecoming their junior year. Of course that was before he'd had his talk with Dad and realized falling in love, making a commitment, meant giving up on his dreams. Something he had no intention of ever allowing.

"I didn't date in high school because no one asked," she said.

"If you drop this whole interview thing, we could go on a date." It had been a while since he'd dated anyone. Dating did not equal commitment.

"You promised to tell me why you have a bodyguard," she said briskly. "And why did you think the ambulance crash wasn't an accident?"

So much for dating her. "Someone's trying to kill me."

## Books by Terri Reed

### Love Inspired Suspense

### Love Inspired

## TERRI REED

At an early age Terri Reed discovered the wonderful world of fiction and declared she would one day write a book. Now she is fulfilling that dream and enjoys writing for Love Inspired Books. Her second book, *A Sheltering Love,* was a 2006 RITA® Award finalist and a 2005 National Readers' Choice Award finalist. Her book *Strictly Confidential,* book five in the Faith at the Crossroads continuity series, took third place in the 2007 American Christian Fiction Writers Book of the Year Award, and *Her Christmas Protector* took third place in 2008. She is an active member of both Romance Writers of America and American Christian Fiction Writers. She resides in the Pacific Northwest with her college-sweetheart husband, two wonderful children and an array of critters. When not writing, she enjoys spending time with her family and friends, gardening and playing with her dogs.

You can write to Terri at P.O. Box 19555, Portland, OR 97280. Visit her on the web at www.loveinspiredauthors.com, leave comments on her blog, www.ladiesofsuspense.blogspot.com, or email her at terrireed@sterling.net.

# TREACHEROUS SLOPES

## TERRI REED

**HARLEQUIN**® LOVE INSPIRED® SUSPENSE

 LOVE INSPIRED BOOKS

ISBN-13: 978-0-373-67594-4

TREACHEROUS SLOPES

Copyright © 2014 by Terri Reed

www.Harlequin.com

**Printed in U.S.A.**

Delight yourself also in the Lord,
and He shall give you the desires of your heart.
—*Psalms* 37:4

Thank you to my family
for always believing in me, Leah Vale for
keeping me from embarrassing myself, and
my editors for all the support and encouragement.

# ONE

"Welcome to this evening's segment of *Northwest Edition.* I'm Julie Frost reporting to you live from the annual Festival of Snow in beautiful Bend, Oregon. It's a crisp Friday night and a perfect way to start the weekend. The festival is proud to host the U.S. Aerial Freestyle National Championship. Excitement is in the air."

Julie kept her gaze on the round, black lens of the handheld camera in front of her. The temperature had dipped below ten on this January evening. Though she'd lived in central Oregon all her life, she couldn't remember it being this cold. Her smile felt frozen in place, like her toes. She should have worn thicker socks. Or boots made for the cold, not fashion. The station stylist had insisted the pink boots matching the pink ski suit completed the outfit. She felt like a big, pink lollipop. The price she paid to be on camera. She refrained from stomping her feet and settled for wiggling her freezing toes. It didn't help.

"As you can see around me, quite a crowd has turned out for the festivities."

She paused as Bob, her cameraman, panned the area, giving their viewers at home a glimpse of what they were missing. The Festival of Snow was held across the Deschutes River from the Old Mill shopping center. The mill with its three towering smoke stacks had been converted into a popular sporting-goods store and provided the anchor to the center. On this side of the footbridge, along the river path, white tents and canopies gave local vendors and artisans warm, dry places to show off their wares while local eateries tempted festivalgoers with tasty treats. A live band played in the amphitheater opposite the wooden structure erected for the skiing competition.

Every year more and more tourists traveled to the mountain oasis to attend the annual festival celebrating the best of winter in Oregon.

When the lens focused back on her, she smiled and raised her voice. She hoped the viewing audience was able to hear her over the cheers of spectators waiting for the aerial freestyle skiers to take to the ramp.

"Tonight's competition is a precursor to

the upcoming winter games. Athletes will compete for points as well as a cash purse of twenty thousand dollars. Points for each jump will be added to the skiers' total season score. Names of the team members representing the U.S.A. at the winter Olympic games will be announced in one week. That will give the athletes two weeks to prepare before traveling to this year's games host city, where they will represent the U.S.A. and compete for gold, silver and bronze."

Julie's gaze slipped to Bob. He nodded encouragingly and made a rolling motion with one hand, letting her know to keep stalling as they waited for the first skier to take his jump.

"Behind me is a specially constructed snow ramp known as a 'kicker.' The skiers will perform two jumps consisting of single or multiple somersaults with or without twists. Each jump must vary by one somersault or one twist. Points are awarded for takeoff, form in the air, difficulty and landing."

Bob motioned with his hand, indicating the competition was starting.

Bubbles of excitement knocked against her ribs. Though she wasn't daring enough to ever try aerial freestyle skiing, she certainly enjoyed watching. It took a risk-taking, adrenaline-junkie personality to pursue a sport where you launched yourself off a fourteen-foot-tall ramp, performed flips and twists fifty feet above the ground, and then landed upright on a steep incline.

Unfortunately, Julie was drawn to that exact type of man. Drawn to and burned by them. She'd had her fill of men who lived life on the edge. Her ex-fiancé had been that sort of man. Only trouble was John Mateo hadn't limited his risky behavior to sports. Thankfully, she'd found out before she'd married him.

Never again would she allow herself to get swept into a relationship with an adrenaline junkie. Next time around—if there was a next time—she wanted stable and steady. Until then she would focus on her career.

Her first step had been convincing her boss at the television station to give her a shot at moving up from production assistant to on-camera personality. The second step had been successfully pitching the idea of a feature story on one of Bend's local heroes, aerial freestyler Nick Walsh, to her boss. He'd said yes. Then she'd contacted Nick's biggest sponsor, Thunderbird Ski Equipment and Apparel, figuring the best way to gain access to Nick would be through his sponsor. The head of the locally based sports company had enthusiastically embraced the idea and looked forward to the promotional aspects of the story. Now all she had to do was put together an excellent story and she'd be given the promotion she craved.

To the camera she said, "Hometown favorite Nick Walsh is taking his position."

When the camera swung away to zoom in on the tall, broad-shouldered skier readying himself at the top of the ramp, a flare of feminine awareness made a joke of her being career-focused. And worse yet, there was so much more to Nick than his good looks.

With a shake of her head, she reminded herself what the story was as the camera came back to focus on her. "Early last year calamity struck the Walsh family when Cody Walsh, Nick's younger brother, had a horrible accident during a practice and died."

Her heart ached for the family. She remembered Cody as a sweet kid who worshipped his older brother.

"The Walsh brothers were taking the aerial freestyle world by storm and were poised to vie for gold against each other as well as the world's top aerialists. Many people speculated Nick wouldn't continue to compete when he dropped out of sight for several weeks after the tragedy." One of the topics she planned to cover later when she interviewed him.

"However, Nick did return to compete and is leading in men's aerials." Recalling the phone conversation she'd had with Nick's manager a few hours ago, she said, "According to Nick's manager, Gordon Lewis, Nick will be performing a new trick for us tonight. One he hopes will take him all the way to gold in the biggest competition of his life!"

A roar for the hometown favorite went up from the crowd. Even as a kid, Nick's one and only passion had been skiing. He'd had his eyes set on winning gold one day. This could be his year.

Bob pointed toward the ramp.

Julie turned to watch, stomping her feet to stay warm, her gaze riveted to the skier waiting to take off. Walsh wore the U.S. team's bright blue-and-red ski suit. Though she couldn't see his face, she had no trouble remembering his vivid blue eyes, thick dark hair and strong jawline.

They'd grown up together, attended the same school and church all the way through to graduation. While she'd been the geeky girl who sat in the front of class, he'd been the one everybody gravitated to at the back. The guys tried to emulate him and failed;

the girls vied for his attention and failed. Including her.

She doubted he'd remember her at all.

Nick Walsh flexed his legs, readying his muscles. He took deep calming breaths. The crowd's roar of expectation lifted on the chilly evening air. Floodlights illuminated the smooth ramp and pooled in a bright circle highlighting the landing track and outrun twenty feet below. A wiser man would resist the urge to scan the crowd for a glint of steel, the small black hole that would put him out of his misery once and for all.

But he wasn't wise.

However, he was definitely unnerved.

This morning he'd received a menacing note—letters cut from a magazine to form three words—*TIME TO DIE*.

After the failed attempt on his life a few months ago, it was little wonder he was edgy.

A flash of color snagged his gaze. A woman stood slightly apart from the rest of the onlookers. Dressed from head to toe in neon pink, she looked like a highlighter except for a long blond braid draped over one shoulder. He blinked and forced himself to focus, which took all his mental prowess considering the death threat looming in the shadows like a mountain lion that roamed the Cascades waiting for an opportune moment to pounce.

Tonight was about testing out a new trick. And moving closer to achieving his goal of medaling in the upcoming games. For Cody.

Nick's heart twisted in his chest.

He concentrated his energy into the moment, blocking out the noises of the spectators and the grief that stabbed at him with each breath. Blocking out the fact that he was back home in the place where his dreams of gold had been born. Blocking out the knowledge that his parents wouldn't be among the audience watching the competition. They still blamed him for Cody's death.

His jaw clenched. He blamed himself.

"Go!"

Heart pumping with adrenaline, Nick pushed off. Pointing his skis down the inrun slope, he picked up speed. He needed to reach thirty miles per hour for optimum liftoff. He approached the kicker. He had to hit it just right to get the height required to perform the quad back, double twist. Wind whipped over his helmet, whistling through the face-mask. Keeping his gaze focused upward, he lifted his arms overhead to elongate his body, increasing his rotational inertia by moving more of his weight away from his hips and allowing for more flipping power.

The approach was perfect.

Wait. Something didn't feel right. His left boot slipped slightly against the toehold.

Someone had messed with his ski and loosened the binding. Sabotage!

His stomach clenched with anticipation and dread. He forced himself to remain calm. He could pull this off.

He hit the kicker and pushed off, soaring high into the air. Momentum carried him up and backward. The blur of stars in the clear night sky appeared like a comet's trail. He arched and gyrated his hips in a hula type move, beginning his first back twist.

His left ski detached from his boot, hitting his arm. Pain ricocheted through the bone. Shock seized his lungs.

The sensation of flying that normally brought him joy sent a shaft of terror shredding through him.

A ripple of panic snatched his breath.

"Help me, God!"

Forget about keeping his body in alignment for the judges. He focused his gaze on the ground, estimating the distance. This wasn't the first time a trick had gone wrong.

He prayed it wouldn't be his last trick ever.

He had to land this in one piece. An injury could knock him out of the competition. He didn't want to wait another four years for the opportunity to go for gold!

He raised his arms overhead to slow his momentum. Pain screamed down his left side from the point of impact with the ski. He elongated his frame, keeping his knees soft and braced himself for the ground.

He hit the landing track with a jarring thud. For a heartbeat, he thought he'd maintain his upright position on the one ski. Then he tumbled, head over end, landing with bruising force against the track and sliding rapidly toward the barrier of the outrun. He curled to protect himself and hit the barrier like a ball bouncing off pavement.

The air left his lungs in a gush and stars danced before his eyes.

He prayed his dreams of gold weren't dead like his brother.

Shrieks of horror splintered the air. Nick's unattached ski flew into the bright orange safety net. He lay in a heap, butted up against the outrun barrier. The cries of the spectators echoed through Julie, heightening her own shock. Reality TV in the flesh.

"Lord, please don't let him be dead."

She did not want to gain ratings by streaming live the death of one of Oregon's—and the country's—favorite skiers. What would this accident to do his chances of competing in February? Would an injury force him to wait four more years or take him out of the running for gold forever by ending not only his career but also his life?

Sympathy and dread knotted her stomach.

Uniformed people and other skiers rushed to Nick's side.

Bob's hand gripped Julie's elbow. "Come on, get in there."

She blinked, letting his words sink in. Right. She had a job to do. Shaking off the shock, she pushed her way through the crowd. "Excuse me. Let us through."

She reached the barrier and flashed her press badge to the man guarding the makeshift gate. He pulled aside the wire mesh so she and Bob could move closer to where Nick lay on the ground. Even though they weren't on the mountain, two Mt. Bachelor ski patrols wearing black snowsuits with bright white crosses on the shoulders attended to Nick. One checked Nick's vitals and the other positioned a toboggan so they could lift him onto the sled.

Julie inched closer but was halted by a

large muscled man in a black ski suit. "Stay back, ma'am."

As she peered around the man, dread curled in her belly. She hated seeing anyone hurt, let alone someone she knew.

Nick moaned and rolled onto his back.

Julie breathed out a sigh of relief.

"Whoa! Slow down," one of the ski patrol said.

"What happened?" Nick asked, coming up on his elbows.

"You took a nasty spill," Julie answered. The pressure in her chest eased. He hadn't broken his neck like his brother. Though she hadn't witnessed Cody's fatal accident, the stories of the event painted a harrowing tale.

Nick reached up and pulled his goggles down past his chin so they hung around his neck. "Do I know you?"

Her heart did a little leap. She smiled but was prevented from answering when the ski patrol stepped between them. "Sir, we're going to lift you onto the toboggan and take you to the clinic tent while we wait for an ambulance."

Nick shook his head. "I don't need to go to the hospital."

"Nick!" A tall man wearing a long wool coat over a double-breasted suit and wing tips shoved his way through the crowd. "Are you hurt? Oh, man, tell me you're not hurt!"

"No, I'm good," Nick said and sat up.

"Sir, please, let's get you onto the toboggan," the ski patrol insisted.

Waving off the guy, Nick said, "No way. I can go on my own two feet." He rolled to all fours and then rose.

A cheer erupted from the crowd.

Nick wobbled. Julie reached out to steady him, along with everyone else. "Stubborn man," she muttered.

He grinned at her. "You don't know the half of it."

"You need to be checked out ASAP!" the well-dressed man exclaimed, looking a little green. "You can't have an injury this close to the games."

"I'm fine. Relax," Nick insisted.

"I won't relax until the doctors say you're fine," the man shot back.

Two skiers, wearing ski suits matching Nick's, positioned themselves on either side of Nick. The Thunderbird logo graced the back of Nick's ski suit, distinguishing him from the other two. The muscled man in black fell in step behind them.

"Come on, dude," the guy on the right said. "Let's get you to the doctor."

They half carried him toward the Mt. Bachelor medical clinic tent set up nearby.

Julie blinked and forced herself to remember why she was there. She turned to face Bob and stared into the camera. "Nick Walsh, ladies and gentlemen. Undoubtedly one of the best aerial freestyle skiers in the country. Not many people could have dropped fifty feet in the air and walked away to ski again."

She prayed that last bit was true. The country was counting on him doing the U.S. proud by medaling.

"Come on," she said to Bob and followed Nick toward the urgent-care tent.

"Nick!" a woman in the crowd called out. "Nick, are you okay? It's me, Kitty."

Nick didn't acknowledge the female's cry.

Julie wasn't sure which of the numerous women pressing up against the barrier had called out. A girlfriend?

"Get a shot of the crowd," she instructed Bob.

As soon as he finished panning the crowd, she hurried around the corner of the urgent-care tent. She hustled so she was in front of Nick and his entourage.

Nick stopped, forcing his companions to do the same. "Jules, is that you?"

Surprise, closely followed by pleasure,

rushed through her, heating her cheeks. "Hey, Nick." She gave herself a mental shake. *Do your job!* She thrust the microphone toward him. "Do you know what went wrong?"

He gave her a lopsided grin. "That wasn't meant to be a monoskiing trick."

"Any idea why your ski came off?"

He tried to sidestep by her, his expression darkening. "I have ideas."

Frustrated that he wouldn't share, she moved into his path. "Will you be doing a second run?"

"No, I won't tonight." He zigged to go around her, taking his buddies with him.

Disappointed he wasn't giving her more, she zagged.

His blue eyes flashed with annoyance, but his smile stayed in place.

"We're glad you weren't hurt," she stated into the microphone.

"Me, too." He tried again to move past her.

Knowing she'd have his attention during the interview and she wouldn't be so easily dismissed, she acquiesced and stepped back. "I'm looking forward to interviewing you later."

His smile faltered. "No interviews."

"Nick Walsh. What a kidder you are!" she quipped into the microphone, trying to salvage the live shot and keep it on a positive tone.

Staring at his retreating back, Julie pressed her lips together. The interview had been arranged. She'd been assured Nick would cooperate. Obviously he hadn't been informed yet.

Gathering her composure, she plastered on a smile and turned back to the camera. "Exciting turn of events tonight at the Festival of Snow. But thankfully Nick Walsh is unharmed. I will be interviewing him later for a special segment of *Northwest Edition*. Stay tuned."

Julie made a cut motion with her hand, indicating for Bob to cut the feed, then ducked through the tent flaps. Inside the clinic tent, welcome warmth seeped through her, making her limbs tingle. There were several screens lined up to cordon off makeshift exam rooms.

A woman seated behind a table glanced up. "Can I help you?"

"Nick Walsh."

"Excuse us!" An elderly man elbowed his way past Julie. "My wife is having trouble breathing."

The woman jumped up and came around the table to help the man with the pale older woman. "Let's get you settled over here."

She glanced distractedly at Julie and pointed toward the farthest screen.

"Your husband's behind curtain number three."

Julie drew back. "Oh, I'm—"

The woman turned her back, cutting Julie off as she led the older couple toward an exam table.

Julie hesitated for a moment, not comfortable letting the woman believe she was Nick's wife, but seeing no opportunity to correct her, she walked away in search of Nick.

Voices raised in argument directed the way. She stopped just inside the screen barrier.

"I didn't pass out," Nick said, his voice raspy with irritation. He'd removed his goggles and helmet and sat on an exam table. Though he looked older than the last time she'd seen him in person, he was still handsome, even when pale and grouchy. "I had the wind knocked from me, that's all."

"Doesn't matter," the well-dressed man insisted. "You're going to the local hospital for a head scan. The doctor agrees. He's arranging it now."

"I don't need the hospital!"

"We already know he's not right in the head," said one of the skiers who'd helped him from the arena. He had blond hair badly in need of a trim and a scraggly beard that was so popular with guys under thirty.

"The scan will only prove it," the other skier, who had light brown hair and brown eyes, joked.

"What are you two still doing in here?" the well-dressed man snapped. "Get out there and do your jumps. I can't have all three of you out of the competition!"

Slipping past Julie with curious glances, the two skiers beat a hasty retreat.

Nick shrugged out of the top layer of his ski suit. A dark purple bruise covered his left arm starting below his elbow, spreading up his biceps and disappearing beneath his Dri-FIT T-shirt. Julie gasped at sight of his injury.

The big man in black, who had his back to her, swiveled and blocked her path.

Nick's eyes widened. "No, it's okay. Let Jules through." Then a slow smile curved his mouth. "I never turn away a beautiful woman. Especially one in head-to-toe pink."

Heat crept into her cheeks, but she refused to respond to his comment.

The well-dressed man moved closer to inspect Nick's bruised skin. "Is your arm broken? Please tell me it's not broken. You can't compete with a broken arm!"

"No, it's not broken," Nick said, bending

his arm on a wince. His gaze zeroed on his manager. "Gordon, you need to find the ski—" Nick flicked a quick glance at Julie. He seemed to hesitate a moment before saying, "Check the binding."

"Is that what caused the ski to fall off, a faulty binding?" she asked.

Gordon stared at her for a moment as if just noticing her. "How did you get back here?"

"It's been a long time, Jules," Nick said, drawing her attention. He held his injured arm close to his body and looked as if he were about to topple over.

Concerned, she moved to sit next him so she could grab him if he pitched sideways. "Yes. Yes, it has."

"You two know each other?" Gordon asked, his gaze bouncing between them.

"Yep. Grew up together." Nick grinned.

She held out her hand to Gordon. "Julie Frost, *Northwest Edition*."

Dawning realization widened Gordon's hazel eyes. "Right." He shook her hand. "Gordon Lewis, Nick's manager. We spoke earlier."

"Nice to meet you."

*"Northwest Edition?"* Nick asked. "As in the TV show?"

"I've been working there since college,"

she said, which was technically true. She didn't mention her official job title was production assistant. If all went well with the story on Nick, she'd be hosting her own segment by the end of the month.

"So Jules, how *did* you get back here?"

She grimaced guiltily as she answered Nick's question. "The woman manning the table out there thought I was your wife."

His eyebrows twitched. "Not that I wouldn't mind, but you're a reporter. I'd never date, let alone marry, a reporter."

Bristling, she stared at him. "Excuse me?"

A doctor wearing a white lab coat over ski pants entered with a wheelchair. "Mr. Walsh, a transport will be here shortly to take you to St. Charles Memorial Medical Center." He moved to inspect Nick's arm. "Let's get an X-ray of your arm," the doctor said. "In the chair, please."

Julie stepped back as Gordon and the doctor helped Nick into the wheelchair. The doctor rolled him out of the exam room, the big guy in black following closely behind. Julie figured he must be event security.

She turned to Gordon. "What will happen if there is a break in his arm or the CT scan shows a brain injury?"

"There would be no possibility of competing in the upcoming winter games." Gordon ran a hand through his hair, clearly freaked out by Nick's close call. "I can't believe this is happening. We're so close."

"It's been a hard year for Nick," Julie stated quietly.

His weary gaze met hers. "For us all, Ms. Frost."

"If Nick is knocked out of the running for a spot on the U.S. ski team, who do you think the committee would choose?"

Gordon shrugged. "There are thirteen skiers from the B and C teams ready and willing to step into his place on the A team, including the two skiers who were just here. And more behind them that would jump at the chance to be invited to join the U.S. ski team."

Julie ached for Nick. She could only imagine how devastated he'd be if an injury this close to the games took him out of the competition.

"I take it you didn't tell him about the interview," she said, still smarting by Nick's comment that he wouldn't date or marry a reporter. Not that she wanted to date him—or marry him—but still…

Gordon winced. "I didn't have time. But I will, once we know he's okay."

She let out a dry scoff. "I get the distinct impression he won't be pleased."

"Probably not, but he'll do it. I'll make sure of it."

"What does he have against reporters?"

Gordon sighed. "After the way the media smeared Cody's reputation with nasty accusations about drugs and alcohol usage causing his death, Nick's not too trusting of the press."

A twinge of unease twisted her tummy.

She hadn't believed the reports of drug use leading to the accident that took Cody's life and had thought the media storm had been unfair to a man who wasn't there to defend himself.

It was important she convince Nick not to paint her with the same brush. Her promotion, her career, rode on his cooperation.

But did she have the skills necessary to succeed?

# TWO

The doctor returned without Nick. Julie's heart leaped to her throat. "Is Nick okay?"

Nodding, the doctor said, "There's no fracture. Only a bruise, but that will heal over time. The transport's here. The ski patrol is getting him onboard. Are either of you going with him?"

"I am," Gordon stated.

Seeing an opportunity for a moment alone with Nick to pursue her story, Julie tapped Gordon on the shoulder. "Your other skiers need you."

Gordon hesitated, clearly torn between his duty to Nick and his duty to his other clients.

"I'll go with Nick," she offered. "You come to the hospital as soon as you can. There's nothing you can do for him right now anyway. Right?"

Clearly relieved, Gordon said, "I'd appreciate it. I'll okay it with the EMTs. If Nick gives you any hassle, you tell him I said *don't*."

After hastily explaining to Bob where she was going and having his assurance he'd follow in the news van, Julie rushed to the ambulance. Since Nick wasn't critical, only one EMT was present for the drive to the hospital. She climbed into the bay of the ambulance and sat on the metal bench.

The big guy in black stopped in the doorway. "Hey, what are you doing?"

Nick lay on the gurney. He blinked at her. "Yeah, what *are* you doing?"

"Filling in for Gordon. He needs to stay for your buddies." She directed her answer to Nick rather than to the security guard.

"Mr. Walsh?" Big guy's tone held a note of displeasure.

"It's fine. Sit up front, Ted."

Ted gave her a censuring look before closing the back bay doors.

"Why is event security going to the hospital with you?" Julie asked.

"He's not with the event. He's my personal security," Nick answered.

Her interest piqued, she asked, "Personal security? Like a bodyguard?"

"Yes. Lots of athletes hire personal protection. Fans, you know." He slanted her a glance. "I'm sure he's not happy with you back here."

"You don't need to worry, I won't bite," Julie teased.

One corner of Nick's mouth twitched. "I might."

"I don't think you're in any shape to be a threat to me."

"You never know." He closed his eyes for a moment. His jaw tensed. "I wish the doc could have given me something for the pain."

"He didn't because they need to know if you're loopy because you smacked your head, not because of meds." She couldn't resist smoothing back a lock of his dark hair from his forehead.

His eyes popped opened, his expression inscrutable.

Afraid of making the wrong move and messing up this opportunity, she tucked her hands into the pockets of her pink ski jacket. "Your arm's not broken, which is good."

As if she'd picked back up some sort of gauntlet she'd thrown down between them, he closed his eyes again and sighed. "Hmm, hmm."

For a long moment, the sound of the ambulance's tires crunching over the gravel put down on the roads to provide traction filled the bay. Julie was content to look at him. She hadn't seen him in the flesh since high school graduation. And even then it had been from a distance.

"You look good," he said, startling her. "Great smile. No more braces."

"I haven't had braces since I was fifteen." Was that how he remembered her?

"Hmm. Long time ago."

When she didn't respond, he opened one eye. "You're still here."

"I'm not going anywhere."

He smiled and closed his eyes. "I meant Bend."

"Yeah, well—"

"Hey! Watch out!" Ted yelled from the front of the ambulance.

The ambulance veered sharply. The tires squealed. Julie yelped as the force of the sudden swerve pitched her forward. She landed sprawled across Nick's chest.

His uninjured arm came around her back, holding her tight. "Steady now."

Gripping the sides of the gurney, Julie lifted her head, her face inches from his. "What was—"

"Hang on!" the EMT driver shouted.

The vehicle decelerated rapidly.

The force of the unexpected speed change

threw Julie forward again until her face was buried in the crook of Nick's neck. His good arm pinned her to his chest. The ambulance came to a sudden halt, the sound of crunching metal echoing in her ears. The contents of the ambulance rained down on them.

"Mr. Walsh!" Ted's frantic cry pierced through the echo of the crash ringing in Julie's ears.

She lifted her head and stared at a wide-eyed Nick. "You okay?"

"Yes. You?"

"I think so."

Every point of contact between her and his muscled chest and strong arm registered in her stunned brain. Warmth crept up her neck and flooded her face.

"You sure? You look a little rattled," Nick said. "Like you could use some reassurance."

"Yes. What? No, I—"

The back bay doors flew open. Julie jerked upright, pushing herself off Nick.

Ted loomed in the doorway. "Mr. Walsh?"

Nick lifted his head. "We're good in here." His gaze narrowed with a hard glint. "What happened?"

"Idiot driver cut us off. We hit a patch of ice and slammed into a telephone pole."

"You think it was an accident?" Nick asked.

Julie slanted Nick a curious glance. Why would he think it wasn't?

"Can't be sure. Guy didn't stop."

Nick dropped his head back. "Get us out of here."

"On it, sir," Ted said and closed the doors.

"What's going on?" Julie asked, feeling as though she'd somehow stepped in the middle of a scene without a script.

Nick closed his eyes. "I'll explain later. Provided I make it to the hospital in one piece."

"You will," she promised and pushed his hair off his forehead again, feeling protective and attracted all at the same time. And why not? The man was gorgeous.

Granted, as a kid he'd always been cute, with his hair flopped over his forehead in a sort of roguish way that had made more than one young girl's heart flutter.

Okay, *her* young heart.

The man before her was even more handsome than the boy he'd been. Time and years spent outdoors had etched lines on his face that enhanced his rugged good looks, making him appear mature and wild at the same time.

And yes, sent her adult woman's heart pounding.

*So* not the appropriate reaction to be having for the subject of the story she wanted to tell. She would not, could not, let the attraction flaring within her have any room. He was so far from the type of man she needed in her life. Most important, if she wanted that promotion, she needed to put anything other than professionalism in a tight box and stuff it deep down in a place where it wouldn't interfere with her career goal.

Only trouble was she had a feeling being the perfect professional would be easier said than done.

A second ambulance arrived and Nick was transferred to the back. At the hospital, Nick and his guard went with the medical personnel. Julie was stopped at the swinging doors.

"Are you his wife?" a nurse asked. "Or sister?"

"Friend."

"Sorry, family only," the nurse said, giving her a sympathetic smile. "You can go to admitting and they can let the patient know you're here."

Waiting wasn't Julie's biggest strong suit, but she had no choice. She quietly prayed that the tests would come back negative. It would be a horrible shame if he wasn't fit to compete in three weeks.

Bob appeared at her side and took the seat

next to her. "Are you okay? I was following the ambulance when it crashed."

"A little shaken up," she replied. "Did you see what happened?"

"Yeah, that car passed me and then cut in front of the ambulance. Next thing I know the ambulance is swerving and *bam,* into the pole. I got some footage of the banged-up ambulance and of them transferring Nick to the second ambulance."

She bit her lip. Knowing how Nick felt about the press, she doubted he'd be okay with them airing the videotape. But it would add so much to the feature. *Injured skier's ambulance crashes.* The public would go nuts for it. Especially with the film of Nick's ski accident and him getting to his feet to walk away from the crash. It would build him up even more as a legend and hero to the American people. And if—when—he won gold next month, it would be even better.

Deciding whether to use the film or not would be a bridge she'd have to cross eventually, but for now she'd say a prayer for Nick's health and hope that when the time came to make that decision it would be easy.

Bob chitchatted with her about mundane matters as they waited. She appreciated his calming presence. Ten years older than she,

Bob had taken her under his wing when he found out she had aspirations of being on camera. He'd worked with her, getting her comfortable in front of the lens.

He'd become a good friend. They made a good team.

An hour later, Gordon joined them in the waiting area.

Julie set down the magazine she was reading and stood. "Have you seen him?"

Looking tired and worn, Gordon said, "Yes. The docs are done. There was no sign of a brain injury."

Julie let out a little sigh of relief. "Have you contacted his parents?"

"Yes. I let them know he's fine."

"I'm sure they're relieved. Can I see him?"

"As soon as the neurologist cleared him, they gave him something for the pain. He's a bit groggy. They'll release him in a bit."

Julie glanced at Bob. He pointed to his camera. She read his message clearly. He wanted to film Nick in his room. It would add a nice dimension to what they already had on tape. She turned her attention back to Gordon. "Could we get a little footage of him in his hospital bed?"

Gordon frowned. "Not right now. Maybe when he wakes."

"I'll be here." Resigning herself to waiting, she sat back down as Gordon returned to Nick's room.

"I'm going for coffee," Bob said. "Want some?"

"Please." She settled back to look through another magazine. "If I'm not here, come find me in Nick's room."

He saluted and sauntered off with his camera, which he never let out of his sight.

A few minutes later a woman took a seat a couple chairs away from Julie. She was pretty with dark hair and dark eyes and held a gift-wrapped box in her hands. Something about her seemed familiar, but Julie couldn't place from where. She exchanged a smile with her and went back to reading.

A nurse stepped into the waiting area.

"Are you here to see Nick Walsh?"

"Yes," Julie said.

"Yes," the brunette said at the same time.

The nurse looked as confused as Julie felt. Eyeing the brunette closely, Julie realized why she'd recognized her. She'd been the one calling out to Nick after his crash.

"Uh, tell me your names and I'll let him know you're both here," the nurse said, clearly uncomfortable letting two women in to see Nick when he was only expecting one.

"Julie Frost."

"Kitty Rogers," the brunette stated. "He'll see me."

Julie arched an eyebrow at the woman's certainty. Clearly she had some claim on Nick. Something unpleasant stirred in Julie's tummy. She mentally stopped herself in her tracks. She needed to remain professional. Knowing he had a girlfriend would help to keep her own feelings in check. She would never poach another woman's man.

Even if that man had had the starring role in her girlhood daydreams.

Nick shifted uncomfortably on the hospital bed. Though he appreciated the excellent medical care he was receiving from Bend's premier medical center, he wanted to be back on the slopes hitting the kicker, not confined to an eight-by-ten room with linoleum floors, stucco walls and the smell of antiseptics filling his head.

The memory of the fresh floral scent of Julie's perfume tightened his gut. She'd smelled like a warm, sunny spring day.

Julie.

The image of a pretty blonde danced through Nick's mind. She'd been Julie Tipton when he'd known her. Man, she'd blossomed, becoming a beautiful woman sans the glasses or the braces he remembered. She'd always been the quiet, studious type. Not the kind to go into show business.

She'd saved his bacon a few times in high school when he'd asked her for help with his English assignments and his math homework. The girl had been wicked smart. Now she was a newshound. A reporter. Go figure.

Distaste coated his mouth. He didn't like the press. Didn't like the way they sensationalized or capitalized on every aspect of his and his fellow athletes' lives, the good and the bad. Whatever would generate ratings was fair game.

Just look at the way they'd sensationalized Cody's death.

Familiar pain and grief welled until he thought he'd drown.

Gordon entered his hospital room. Tight lines of concern bracketed his eyes and mouth. "Doc says you're A-OK. They'll release you in few hours."

"Sweet."

"We have a lot riding on you being fine," Gordon reminded him.

*We* being Gordon and the sponsors backing Nick. The biggest of which was an international company with its headquarters in Bend and named after one of the runs on Mt. Bachelor. The CEO of Thunderbird had supported Nick even after Cody's death last year and had continued to provide financial support during the weeks when Nick was too grief stricken to train, let alone compete.

Nick owed them big-time.

And he always repaid his debts.

"Ted tell you about the ambulance ride?" His heart thumped remembering the chaos. And Jules. The smell of her hair, the way her bright blue eyes had flared with first shock, then concern and finally awareness before she'd shot away as though she'd been burned.

"He did. He gave the police a good description of the car." Worry darkened Gordon's hazel eyes. "I don't like this."

"You and me both. Whoever sent that threatening note is going to a lot of trouble to hurt me."

"That's why it's important Ted stay close," Gordon said. "And that you cooperate and let him do his job keeping you safe."

Nick had every intention of staying safe and alive.

"Hey, there's something else I need to tell you," Gordon said.

"They found the ski?" Nick asked.

"Yes. Given the circumstances, the local

police have taken charge of it and sent the ski to the crime lab for inspection."

Nick's fingers curled into a fist. There was no doubt in his mind this hadn't been an accident but another attempt on his life.

"But that's not what I wanted to talk about," Gordon said, drawing up a chair to the bedside. "The local lifestyle TV show *Northwest Edition* is going to do a feature piece on you."

Nick drew back. "Excuse me?"

Gordon held up his hands like brackets on a marquee. "Local Hero Comes Home for Anniversary of Brother's Death." He shrugged and lowered his hands.

A knife twisted in Nick's gut. "I will not use Cody's death to bolster my career."

"Not just your career. Thunderbird wants the exposure. They are fully on board with Ms. Frost's idea for a feature story on you. This will be good exposure for them."

Nick snorted. "Great. And if I refuse?"

"You can tell Lucas Davenport." Gordon took out his cell phone. "You want me to get him on the line?"

As much as it galled him, Nick shook his head.

Gordon put his phone back in his pocket. "*Northwest Edition* wants to do a human-interest story. Their reporter, Julie, is a sweet gal and easy on the eyes."

"Jules is great," Nick said, figuring better the enemy you know.

"Tell me you didn't break her heart."

Nick scoffed. "Naw. Nothing like that."

She'd been out of his league then. Now she was just plain dangerous. A reporter. His mind struggled to wrap around the concept.

Gordon rubbed his hands together. "Excellent. Local girl, local guy. It's all good."

Gordon was always working the angles. "I don't know about this."

"I worked out a deal with the station manager that we reserve the right to edit the piece or scrap the whole thing if it doesn't meet with our approval. Does that help?"

A small consolation. One he could live with. "I suppose."

"Good. She's waiting to come talk with you," Gordon said. "I told the nurse to give me ten minutes and then send her in."

Nick wasn't surprised to hear she was still at the hospital. She wanted her story. "Oh, by the way, Kitty followed me home to Bend. I saw her in the crowd tonight."

Katherine "Kitty" Rogers, a ski groupie, had been hounding him for the past year. When she'd first starting hanging around the competitions, making it clear she was there to see him, he'd been flattered. Amused, even, the first two or three times she appeared in the crowd. But then it started to creep him out. Last month she'd gone so far as to find his hotel room in Colorado and wait outside his door. She'd made it clear she was willing to be more than just an adoring fan. There was something slightly off about her that made him wary.

Gordon wrinkled his nose. "She's your biggest fan."

"She's taking it to the extreme."

"Excuse me." The nurse stood in the doorway. "There are two women waiting to see you, Mr. Walsh. A Julie Frost and a Kitty Rogers."

Of course Kitty was here. Nick nearly laughed at the irony. "Send in Jules, not Kitty."

The nurse nodded and retreated.

"And the hits just keep on coming," Nick commented dryly.

A few minutes later Julie knocked on the door frame.

"Come on in." Nick drank in the sight of her. The pink color of her outfit heightened the rosy hue of her cheeks and brightened her crystal-blue eyes. Her sleek blond braid made him wonder if she was as tightly coiled. What would she do if he reached out and undid the band holding the strands together?

"I'm glad to see you're feeling better," she said, moving farther into the room.

"Much, thank you." He didn't like being in such a vulnerable position, trapped in bed wearing a hospital gown and totally at a disadvantage with a lovely lady.

"There's a woman out there waiting to see you," Julie said. "Is she your girlfriend?"

"No," Nick said quickly and exchanged a glance with Gordon.

Gordon stood. "Here, sit. I'll take care of that situation."

Nick sent Gordon a grateful nod. He hoped Gordon would be able to send Kitty on her way. There was something in the woman's eyes that gave him the same feeling that had seized him when his boot had shifted in the ski binding today.

Julie took a seat and pulled out a notebook from the big flowered shoulder bag that she dropped at her feet.

So she wanted to get down to business. He watched her slender hands flip open the pad, her pen poised. There was a noticeable lack of a wedding ring. Curious, he asked, "Where's Mr. Frost tonight?"

Julie grinned. "Afraid he'll come storming in, jealous over me being at your bedside?"

"I like to be prepared."

She laughed. "Frost is my stage name. Rolls off the tongue better than Tipton. There's no mister attached to it or me."

"You never married?" He'd figured she'd have found some intellectual at the fancy college she'd surely attended and be happily married by now.

Her gaze dropped to her hands. She fiddled with the pen. A shadow crossed over her face. "No. Never found the right guy."

"Too picky?"

Her gaze shot up to meet his. Indignation flared in the light blue depths. "No. That's not it all. Why would you say that?"

He'd struck a nerve. Which made him more curious and stirred an ache in his chest he couldn't explain. Had someone hurt her? The thought didn't settle well. "I remember in high school you didn't date. I figured you were holding out for a brainiac like yourself." At least that was what he'd told himself when he'd chickened out and didn't ask her to homecoming their junior year. Of course that was before he'd had his talk with Dad and realized falling in love, making a commitment, meant giving up on his dreams. Something he had no intention of ever allowing.

A rueful twist touched her mouth, drawing his gaze again. "I didn't date in high school because no one asked."

He felt like a heel. "I should have asked you."

She looked at him from beneath her lashes. "I would have liked that."

"If you drop this whole interview thing, we could go on a date." It had been a while since he'd dated anyone. Dating did not equal commitment. At least not to him, which was why he rarely dated.

She inhaled sharply. "That would be like asking me to stop breathing, Nick."

"Good thing I know CPR."

She rolled her eyes. "You promised to tell me why you have a bodyguard," she said briskly. "And why did you think the ambulance crash wasn't an accident?"

So much for dating her. "Someone's trying to kill me."

# THREE

Julie's jawed dropped. She snapped it shut as his words reverberated through her brain. Someone was trying to kill Nick?

Her mind reeled. First his talk of dating if she'd drop the feature on him and now this? Nick's story was bigger than she'd ever imagined. Her mind popped with questions. "Why would someone want to kill you? Who wants to kill you? What's happened that would lead you to believe that?"

"Whoa." Nick held up a hand. "Slow down. Shouldn't you be waiting for me to answer one question before you throw me another?"

Her face flamed. "Of course. Yes. Sorry. You're right. Of course, you're right."

He touched her arm. "It's okay. Take a deep breath."

She took in a shuddering breath to calm her racing heart.

"Better?"

"Yes." She poised her pencil over the pad of paper. "Okay. This is huge, Nick. Where's Bob and his camera?" She tapped the pencil against the pad. "I'd like to get a shot of you here in the hospital, if you'd be comfortable with that." From the appalled look on his face, she guessed he wasn't. "Okay, scratch that idea."

"Please do. In fact, let's call the whole interview off."

She searched his face, trying to decide if he was serious. His jaw was set. His eyes flinty. Yep, he was serious. "But we can't. Surely you understand that."

He shook his head. "I'm not thrilled about being the subject of your interview."

"But you will go through with the interview, right?" She hated how desperate she sounded.

His dark blue eyes narrowed. "Why is this so important to you?"

Should she tell him what was at stake? She didn't want to sound whiny or pathetic, but if he understood that her shot at becoming an on-air reporter hinged on how well she delivered this story for *Northwest Edition,* then maybe he'd cooperate. She didn't have anything to lose except her pride.

"This is my first big break. I went out on

a limb and pitched this idea for a feature on you to my boss in hopes of securing a permanent on-camera spot. I can't afford to keep working there if I don't get this promotion."

"So what is your actual job now?"

"I'm a production assistant."

"Ah, okay." Nick repressed the chuckle that bubbled up. No wonder she'd been nervous and overly enthusiastic with her questions. And why she needed the promotion. He doubted being an assistant paid that well. "I'd like to help you, but…"

She sat forward. "Mr. Davenport at Thunderbird was excited about the idea. He said he wanted to make new skin designs for your skis and to unveil them live during the segment." Her voice rose slightly. Her teeth tugged on her bottom lip.

His gaze landed on her mouth. She'd always had perfectly shaped lips. Soft and supple. Kissable. He remembered thinking that in high school. Of course back then her lips had been devoid of lipstick. She'd never been one to wear all that stuff on her face the way most of the teen girls did.

Her lips parted slightly, making him aware he'd been staring.

He could tell this meant a lot to her. But the

anger he'd felt over the media raking Cody through the mud grated something fierce.

She reached to touch his hand. Sympathy tinged her gaze. "I was sorry to hear about Cody's accident. I sent flowers."

Nick's breath hitched. Grief stabbed him. He fought the burning behind his eyes. The place where her fingers rested lightly on his hand created a hot spot, distracting him from the pain stirred up by her words. He hadn't known she'd sent flowers. Of course, he hadn't really been aware of much at the time. "That was thoughtful of you."

A commotion outside the door drew his attention away from the pretty lady sitting beside him.

Ted blocked the doorway.

"But I want to see him!" said a female blocked from Nick's view.

He didn't have to see the woman to recognize Kitty's voice. She was making a scene and disturbing the peace of the hospital. Nick winced. He'd thought Gordon was going to deal with her. Obviously he hadn't been successful.

"That other woman was allowed in," Kitty shrieked. "Nick! Nick, tell this man to let me in."

"Who's she?" Julie asked in a whisper.

"A fan," Nick said. He sighed. Thinking of the other patients, he called out, "Ted, it's okay. I'll see her if it will make her stop fussing."

Ted glanced over his shoulder. "You're sure?"

"Why not? Let's just add to my humiliation."

Julie gave him a chiding look as Kitty barged into the room, carrying a small, wrapped present. She was an attractive woman with dark hair curling around her impish face, wide dark eyes, red lips and a Marilyn Monroe–type mole at the corner of her mouth. He wasn't sure if the detail was real or for effect. She had on well-worn jeans and a red sweater that emphasized her assets. But to Nick, Kitty was a dark shadow compared to the shimmering lightness of Julie. The two couldn't have been more opposite in looks or personality.

"Hello, Kitty," Nick said, trying hard to keep his irritation from showing. "What are you doing here?"

She laughed lightly and shot Julie a curious glance. "You know I come to every one of your competitions that I can. I'm so excited to see your hometown. You gave me quite a scare today. I thought for sure you were going die when that ski flew off." She moved to wedge herself in front of Julie and put one hand on his shoulder. "Are you all right?"

"As you can see, alive and well."

"Then why are you in the hospital?"

"Observation. I'll be leaving soon."

She thrust the gift at him. "I brought you something."

He didn't take it. "That's thoughtful, but you shouldn't have. Really, you shouldn't have."

A steely glint flashed in her eyes. "It's for you."

Apparently she wasn't going to let him refuse. He took the present and quickly unwrapped it to reveal a money clip engraved with his initials and a note telling him where she was staying. As if he'd ever take her up on her propositions. He tucked the money clip back in the box. "Thank you, Kitty."

Julie cleared her throat.

Nick gave Julie an apologetic grimace. "Julie, this is Kitty Rogers. A fan."

Kitty's fingers dug into the top of his shoulder. "His number-one fan."

Julie's speculative gaze bounced from Kitty to Nick to the hand on his shoulder and back to Kitty. "I can see that." She stood and held out her hand, forcing Kitty to relinquish her hold on his shoulder. Nick gave Julie a grateful smile.

"Nice to meet you," Julie said.

"What are *you* doing here?" Kitty asked with barely veiled jealousy.

Julie opened her mouth to respond, but Nick jumped in. "She's with me." He reached past Kitty to take Julie's hand.

Two sets of eyes blinked at him.

"I am?"

"She is?"

He squeezed Julie's hand, hoping she'd go along with the ruse. He needed Kitty to back off. He didn't want her attention. And faking a girlfriend might just be the ticket to sending Kitty scurrying back to Idaho, where she'd come from. "Julie and I are rekindling our relationship."

Julie choked at Nick's words and wished she had a drink of water to wash away her surprise. Nick's eyes implored her to confirm his statement.

The need to back him up compelled her to admit, "We are old friends."

Kitty's eyes narrowed. Shockingly obvious anger flared in the dark depths. "Nick and I are friends, too."

Sensing how uncomfortable the woman

was making Nick, Julie sought to defuse the situation. Most people wanted their fifteen minutes of fame, and Julie counted on Kitty to be no different.

Julie smiled sweetly. "Kitty, I work for *Northwest Edition,* a weekly lifestyle television magazine, and I'm doing a piece on Nick. And because you are his self-professed number-one fan, I'd love to interview you."

For a moment uncertainty crossed Kitty's face, then slowly her demeanor shifted and excitement built in her eyes. "You want to interview me? On TV?"

Ignoring Nick's sudden coughing fit, Julie kept her voice smooth. "Yes. I'd love to have your take on Nick's career and the upcoming games. Nick will be competing in the fiercest contest of his life. I want to explore all the facets of an elite athlete. Including the fans. Maybe you could give me some insight on what it's like to be such a devoted fan?"

Kitty practically glowed. "That would be super."

The possessive-woman bit fell away. Kitty appeared younger than Julie had originally thought when she'd forced her way into Nick's room. Julie slipped a card out of her purse and handed it to Kitty. "Here's my card. Call me and we'll set it up."

"Thank you." Kitty hugged the card to her chest. "Isn't this fabulous, Nick?"

"Fabulous," he repeated dully.

"I can't wait to tell everybody." Kitty hurried away.

Julie wondered who *everybody* was.

"Why did you do that?" Nick asked the second Kitty disappeared out the door. "Don't encourage her."

"It will be fine," Julie assured him. "It will give her an opportunity to talk about you. And she might have some useful insight. Maybe even have some ideas of who would benefit with you out of the way."

"I can name a hundred aerial freestylists who'd benefit, but not one that I could point a finger to and say they're the type to go to those lengths."

She shrugged. "If nothing else, interviewing Kitty will give her something else to focus on."

His intent gaze met hers. "And you'll say we're in a relationship if she asks?"

"If you're doing the interview, then we have a working relationship," Julie stated.

She could see him debating with himself. Finally, he said, "Good enough. Maybe she'll back off." He visibly relaxed. "I owe you."

She smiled. "Then you'll talk with me."

"Talk? You don't want to talk, you want to dissect me like we did those frogs in biology class." He held up a hand. "Oh, wait. I did the dissecting. You couldn't watch."

Her nose wrinkled up. "I still can't look at a frog without gagging." She suppressed a shudder. "You were my hero that day."

An answering grin tugged at the corners of his mouth. "You did turn a nasty shade of green, like I'd never seen before or since."

"Not my finest moment." But it had been worth it since she got to spend time with him. He'd sat in front of her in class. Most days all she saw was the back of his head. But that day…she'd been the envy of the other girls in class when Nick had turned around and asked her to be his partner.

She held his gaze and something indefinable passed between them. A shared past, memories of simpler days. The longing to go back to those days grabbed ahold of her as she lost herself in the blue depths of his eyes. Was that same yearning there in his gaze?

"Wouldn't you rather tell your story to me than someone who doesn't care about you?"

His eyes widened. "You care?"

She touched his arm. "Of course I care. You're a big deal in this town."

"Right." He tapped a finger against his lip

as he contemplated her. Finally, he let out a short laugh. "I'm nuts to agree to this. But you're the only reporter I would ever trust."

Gratified and hoping that his words were a forecast of a successful promotion, she sat in the chair. "You won't regret it."

"We'll see."

"Are you always so skeptical?" She hadn't remembered that from when they were young. She'd considered him to be one of the most laid-back and driven people she knew. The dichotomy was what made him so interesting.

"I've become more so," he stated.

"Mr. Walsh, this man says he's with her," Ted said from the doorway.

Seeing Bob over Ted's shoulder, Julie said, "That's right, he is." She stood. "I should let you get some rest."

He reached for her hand again. "You don't have to run off yet."

His warm palm pressed against hers, making her feel connected to him. She swallowed back the jolt of yearning that grabbed her by the throat. She wanted to feel connected, to be a part of a couple. Had thought she'd found that sort of connection with John, but he'd proved less than trustworthy. She wasn't ready to put her heart on the line again. Especially not with Nick.

Flirting came naturally to a guy like him and meant nothing. She had to remain unaffected by his charm and charisma. She quickly extracted her hand. "It shouldn't be too long before you're released. Besides, Bob is my ride. I can't ask him to wait around."

"We'll drop you off when I'm released," he said. "Or rather, Gordon will since he's the one with the wheels."

As tempting as it was to stay, she shook her head. She needed to keep her perspective. Theirs was a business relationship. She had to remember that and act like the professional she wanted to be. "No. I need to go. I'll be in contact with Mr. Lewis so we can set up a time for you to come to the station for the interview."

His mouth twisted in a rueful way that she found appealing. "You can call me directly. In fact, why don't you come by the motor home tomorrow? You can see how I live when I'm on the road."

Excited by the unexpected invitation to visit his home on wheels, she couldn't help but beam. "That would be great. I'll make sure Bob's free."

Nick's gaze went to the doorway, where Bob waited, and back to her. "Sounds good."

Was that disappointment in his eyes? Couldn't be.

Suddenly reluctant to leave and half afraid he'd change his mind about the invitation tomorrow, she dug out one of her cards and wrote her cell number on the back.

"Here." She thrust the square piece of card stock at him. "Call me with a good time for us to come over."

He took the card, his fingers brushing over hers, setting off little sparks shooting up her arm. She released her hold and backed away. Time to beat a hasty retreat before her resolve to keep their relationship strictly business weakened.

With Julie's departure the room seemed duller and the hospital more oppressive. Nick stared at her business card. It read, "Julie Tipton, production assistant for *Northwest Edition*" and had the call letters of the local affiliate television station. He turned the card over to where she'd written her number in a neat script.

He still couldn't believe it. Julie. Shy, sweet Jules had blossomed into a beautiful, ambitious woman. A reporter. Wannabe. Which made her worse. No doubt she'd do whatever it took to make her story. Including dragging Cody back through the muck.

When she'd said she cared, his heart had sped up, but then she'd clarified that it was because "he was a big deal in this town" and his stomach had dropped as if he'd caught a tip. She was no different than anyone else. He was a ticket to ride. A commodity to exploit. And she wanted her piece.

He couldn't work up the usual animosity he felt when thinking about the press, though. Julie had had his back with the Kitty situation. Even going so far as to prevent a scene by asking Kitty for an interview.

This was one debt that he unexpectedly didn't mind paying.

The next morning, Nick stepped out of the motor home onto the snow-covered ground and filled his lungs with crisp mountain air. The scent of pine teased his senses.

After giving an acknowledging nod to Ted, who'd been waiting outside the door for him, Nick lifted his gaze, drawn by an invisible cord to the snow-capped peak of Mt. Bachelor. The playground of his youth.

The Oregon mountain, part of a string of volcanoes making up the Cascade mountain range, was home to some of the Pacific Northwest's best skiing. It was on these picture-perfect slopes that Nick had learned to ski, learned to love and learned to grieve.

A familiar wave of sorrow and guilt washed over him, bowing his shoulders slightly and making the pressure build in his chest until he thought his ribs would collapse. He forced himself to breathe. His arm throbbed in tempo to the beat of his heart. He sent up a silent thank-you to God that all he'd suffered yesterday was a bruise. He hoped God was listening, because he was going to need His protection.

Whoever wanted him dead had failed this time.

Nick shuddered with certainty that there would be more attempts.

So far the police had had no success finding out who wanted to kill him or why.

Nick had to stay strong and focused. He was so close to realizing the dream he and his younger brother, Cody, had worked their whole lives toward.

Only Cody was gone now. A year ago this coming Thursday. His parents had a one-year anniversary memorial service planned—the reason Nick was staying in town instead of returning to his condo in Lake Placid to await the announcement of who had been chosen to compete in the Winter Games.

Nick hadn't been home since the funeral, because he couldn't bear to see the anguish on his mother's face or the sadness in his dad's eyes.

He'd worked hard this year once he'd gotten his head back in the game after Cody's death. Nick had thrown everything he could into each competition, winning or placing high enough that even without scoring at last night's competition he had earned enough points to qualify for the U.S. team traveling to the games.

He wanted to win gold for Cody.

Nick had a good shot at securing one of the four positions on the U.S. men's aerial team. But so did the other ten U.S. competitors who'd qualified to make the team, including both of his traveling companions.

And Cody would have been among them, too.

The door to the motor home opened behind him and Lee Thompson stepped down and clapped Nick on the back. "Forget your way?"

"Naw, just taking it in." The parking lot adjacent to the West Village Lodge was busy with skiers arriving for a day of fun on this beautiful late-January morning. The sun shone like a bright ball in the clear blue sky and fresh powder dumped sometime in the night glistened in the sun's rays. Perfect conditions for a day on the slopes.

Lee stretched, lifting his arms high and letting out a noisy yawn.

"I'm surprised you're up," Nick stated, noting the dark circles under his teammate's brown eyes.

"Can't waste a beautiful day sleeping."

Lee and Frank had returned to the motor home long after Nick was released from the hospital. The two buddies liked to find the nearest hot social spot and unwind after competing. Nick had always preferred some alone time after a competition.

"You know you and Frank can head back to Lake Placid anytime," Nick said.

Now that last night's qualifier was done, the two men had no reason to stick around Bend.

Lee shot him a sharp look. "We're here for Cody's memorial, too."

They'd loved his brother, as well.

Nick's heart spasmed in his chest.

Cody's death shouldn't have happened. Nick should have prevented Cody from taking that last run.

Despite the way the press had raked Cody's

reputation across the coals with accusations and insinuations, Cody had not been high or drunk. He'd been tired and trying a trick that got away from him.

The burn of anger smoldered in Nick's gut any time he thought about the way the news reporters had spun Cody's accident into something sordid, leaving a taint of speculation blanketing the tragedy.

The image of a blue-eyed blonde marched into his mind. He blew out a breath. He had to trust that Julie would not be made of the same ilk.

"Uh-oh. *Sheeee's baaaack.*" Lee's singsong tone drew Nick's attention.

"Who?"

Mirth danced in Lee's eyes. "Your number-one fan."

She was like a bad penny, showing up unexpected and unwanted.

It occurred to Nick that Kitty's presence had precipitated the last attempt on his life. And she was here now.

Was she somehow involved?

# FOUR

By nine on Saturday morning, Julie had already spent an hour on the elliptical machine in the corner of her living room. After a shower and drying her hair, she put on her robe and slippers and stood inside her walk-in closet trying to decide what to wear. She'd be seeing Nick later today, something she was still having a hard time believing. She wanted to look nice. Professional. Most of her clothes fit into one of two extreme categories: casual or dressy. She had very little in between.

The trill of her cell phone jump-started her heart. She crossed the room and grabbed it off the nightstand. The caller ID revealed a number she didn't recognize. "Hello?"

"Good morning, sunshine."

Nick's deep voice strummed over her senses like a master guitar player. All her nerve endings tingled with alertness. "Good morning to you, too. How's the arm?"

"Still attached," he quipped.

She laughed softly. "That's good."

"Are you available for lunch?"

She sat on the bed. "Lunch?"

"Yeah, you know that meal in the middle of the day. You do eat lunch, don't you?"

"Yes. I'll have to see if Bob's available then," she said.

"How about if Bob arrives after lunch? Say, one o'clock."

He wanted to have lunch with her alone. A little thrill raced down her spine. Not a professional reaction. "I thought you didn't date reporters."

"Oh, so you do want this to be a date?" There was laughter in his tone.

Her cheeks flamed. "No, that's not what I meant."

"I'm game. I'll fix you my mom's famous curry chicken salad."

"You don't have to cook for me."

"I don't have to do anything," he said. "But I'd like to cook for you."

She swallowed back the spurt of very unprofessional pleasure. "I appreciate the offer but—"

"No buts," he said, cutting her off. "Be at the West Village parking lot by eleven-thirty. I'll see you then."

He hung up, giving her no chance to tell him she didn't think it was a wise decision to spend time with him outside of the interview. She stared at the phone. She should dial him back and tell him no.

She didn't. For the sake of her interview, she'd go. Besides, it would help him relax and be ready to open up when Bob arrived with the camera. She had a little over two hours to prepare. Did she have time to buy a new outfit?

*Not a date, remember.* She decided on a knee-length purple skirt, a cream-colored sweater and knee-high low-heeled boots. After twisting her hair and securing the mass with a jeweled clip, she made her way to the second bedroom of the riverfront condo she'd inherited from her mother. They'd lived here before her stepdad, Marshal, came into the picture, but Mom had hung on to the condo. After graduating from college, Julie had moved in. Now it was hers, along with the fees and taxes. She'd turned her old room into a den with a vintage writing desk, an armoire that did double duty as a bookshelf and printing dock and sofa with a standing reading lamp. This room was her haven. She'd repainted the walls herself a light peach and stenciled Scriptures along the top, creating a border so that she was surrounded by God's word as she worked or read. Her laptop lay on the desk.

She sat in the plush custom-made chair Marshal had given her for Christmas several years ago. He'd taken one look at the task chair she'd bought at the local office supply store and decided she couldn't possibly be comfortable in that chair. The task chair had been what she could afford. Having made millions in real estate, it was nothing for Marshal to provide her with a chair. But she wanted to provide for herself. It had been her and her mom alone for so long before Marshal had come along. Her mother had taught her to be strong and independent.

From her purse she took out her notepad. She'd scribbled notes and possible questions when she had first thought of the idea to interview Nick. Now that the time was here, she needed to strategize her interview questions. And she needed to do more research on Nick and his career. She hadn't really followed Nick's rise through the skiing ranks. Of course she'd known he was doing well and had hurt for his family when Cody had his fatal accident. But the first couple of years out of high school had been hard for her with her mother's illness, college and then Mom's passing. That was five years ago. And every day she missed her mom.

The only family she had left was her stepdad. And that relationship was strained at best. Marshal Evans had wanted her to go into real estate so she could take over his business. He'd made it very clear he thought she was wasting her time at the station. But she wasn't interested in selling property any more than she was in taking over his business. She wanted to make her own way in the world. Unfortunately, her salary wasn't cutting it. The promotion would make a huge difference to her financially.

She opened a file folder, labeled *Nick,* that was sitting on the desk. She wanted to know what made him tick.

Because he was the subject of her story, not because she was attracted to him. Okay, maybe she was even after all these years, but that didn't mean she would let her emotions rule her. She was a professional. She had a job to do.

Her thoughts scattered in a million directions.

Who wanted him dead? Why?

Clearly he'd angered someone enough that the person had tried to kill him.

She sent up a silent prayer of protection

for Nick and a plea that whoever wanted him dead would be stopped.

A chill chased down her spine.

She reached over to the sofa and snagged an afghan to throw across her shoulders. Searching the internet, she read every bit of information she could find about Nick Walsh, jotting down more notes as she clicked through the links.

He had a track record of wins that went back to his early teen years. She made a note to ask him about learning to ski on Mt. Bachelor. That was a no-brainer.

He was credited with being one of the sport's most innovative competitors. She could ask about his inspiration both on and off the slopes.

There was an article about a mission trip to India. She made a note to ask about his philanthropic endeavors. And there was a short piece about him guest coaching at a training center back east. Another good topic to cover in her interview.

Of course, she'd focus on the recent attempts on his life. Today at lunch she'd get some specifics and then contact the police investigating the attempts.

She clicked on the images tab and a collage of photos appeared, all featuring Nick.

As a kid, as a teen. The same guy who lived in her memories.

As a young man new on the aerial freestyle roster.

The progression of maturity made her smile.

He'd fulfilled every promise of being a hunk.

There were photos of Nick with ski buddies, two of whom Julie recognized as the men who'd been in the tent with Nick last night.

There were also pictures of Nick with female skiers, both on the slopes and off.

Staring at the images, she thought back to their high school days. He'd been cocky and larger than life, with a grin that made everyone want to respond in kind. That grin hadn't changed over the years and still had the ability to make her catch her breath.

She tagged a few photos and sent them to the production department at the station for use as background.

She made a note that in the articles, there had been no mention of a steady girlfriend.

The curiosity building within her was purely professional. He was an eligible bachelor and her viewers would want to know about his love life.

She called Bob and arranged for him to meet her at Nick's motor home at 1:00 p.m. In a moment of inspiration, she decided to take her tablet, which had a camera. It might just be the two of them in the motor home for lunch, but that didn't mean she couldn't share the experience with the world. She left her condo with purpose in her steps.

When she arrived at the West Village parking lot at the base of Mt. Bachelor, she parked her all-terrain hybrid in an empty slot. She looked toward the West Village Lodge sitting at the rise of a steeply sloped walkway. It had been a while since she'd been to the lodge. Toward the end of her life, Mom had loved to come and sit on the balcony with a mug of hot cocoa and watch Marshal ski.

The bittersweet memory misted Julie's eyes. She blinked to clear away the bout of grief and climbed out of the car. She scanned the lot, looking for Nick's motor home. The RV side of the parking lot was filled with recreational vehicles of all sizes and shapes.

Her gaze landed on a huge RV. That was it. There was no mistaking the Thunderbird logo, a bird depicted in an explosion of color with its wings spread wide and its distinctively shaped head. She set off in that direction.

A shiver of unease shimmied down her

back. The sensation of being watched made the small hairs at the back of her neck rise in an alert tremor. She glanced around. The mostly full lot was busy with people gathering at their cars for tailgate lunches. She didn't see anyone paying special attention to her. Her gaze snagged on the nearest lift ticket booth and the dark-haired woman standing in front of it. She didn't face the window as one would expect, but rather the parking lot. Though the woman was too far away for Julie to make out her features, Julie was sure it was Kitty.

Keeping vigil over Nick?

It would be disconcerting to have someone following you around the country, always showing up and trying to make a connection that wasn't there.

Stalking of celebrities and athletes wasn't a new issue. Bothersome for sure, and in some cases, deadly.

Julie hadn't felt that Kitty was a threat to Nick last night at the hospital. The woman had seemed genuinely concerned about his well-being. Surely Kitty wasn't a danger to anyone. Julie was curious to see if Kitty would actually call and set up an appointment to be interviewed. Sometimes people found the idea of being on camera too nerve-racking to attempt. Julie's first time hadn't been perfect, but she'd loved it.

She turned away from the ticket booth and the woman watching to knock on the motor home door. A second later, it swung open. Ted filled the frame. His intimidating stare softened. "Ms. Frost. Nick's expecting you."

He stepped down and to the side so she could enter.

When he didn't follow her up the stairs, she paused to look back at him. "You're not coming in?"

He flashed her a grin. "Three's a crowd. I'll be out here making sure no one disturbs your lunch." His gaze rose toward where Kitty still stood, staring in their direction.

Julie entered the motor home and the door swung shut behind her. It took a moment for her eyes to adjust. The smell of curry and grilled chicken hung in the air, making her mouth water. Nick stood at the sink in the galley. Light blue jeans fit snugly over his long, lean legs and the teal-colored cable-knit sweater emphasized the width of his shoulders. No sign of a sling. He was chopping a stalk of celery and dropping the bits into a large bowl filled with savory chunks of chicken covered in a yellow curry sauce.

"Hey there, pretty lady," Nick said with a welcoming smile, flashing even, white teeth.

"Hello." She gave him an answering smile. "How's the arm?"

He flexed it. "Still works." He gestured to the dining area. "Have a seat. It's just about ready."

The table had been set up with colorful stoneware plates, utensils, tall tumbler glasses and a pitcher of lemonade.

"Wow, this is great."

The walls were decorated with framed photos of Nick and two other men on the winner podiums. Beneath the photos, the captions stated a date and the name of the competition. Apparently his buddies competed in not only aerials but also moguls and ski cross.

She noticed a box sitting on a shelf with two red baseball caps sporting the Thunderbird logo on the crown and Nick's name embroidered on the bill. "These are cool."

Nick wiped his hands on a towel before stepping over. He lifted the hats out of the box and plopped one on her head and the other on his. "A matching set."

"Does Thunderbird gift you with lots of merchandise?"

"One of the perks of sponsorship." Nick stepped back to the sink. "Every company makes some sort of paraphernalia. These are just hitting the shelves. Though I doubt they all have my name stitched on the peak."

"Nice." She removed the hat from her head and placed it back in the box. Then she scooted onto the cushioned bench seat and placed her tablet on the window ledge, with the camera facing over her shoulder toward the spot where Nick would sit. She pushed record.

He brought the bowl of chicken salad to the table and set it in the middle, then glanced at the tablet. "Is that recording?"

She nodded. "It is okay? I may not use it."

For a moment he contemplated her, then lifted a shoulder. "That's fine."

Relieved, she set her napkin in her lap.

He brought over a stack of pita wedges and loose lettuce leaves. "Help yourself."

Taking one of the wedges, she asked, "What made you decide to concentrate your career on aerials? If I recall you could bomb a hill pretty fast."

He sat on the bench seat to her left and took off the hat to lay it beside him. "I still love to bomb down the slopes. But there's nothing like being a human rocket."

She paused as she scooped a spoonful of

salad onto her plate. "Rocket?" That sounded dangerous.

He took a pita wedge and filled it with lettuce and salad before laying it on the plate. "You fly down the ramp into the jump at forty-plus miles per hour, hit the kicker at a seventy-degree angle, shooting your body upward like a rocket as gravity tries to tether you to the ground, but you're moving up and up and your body's spinning and twisting and twirling."

Exhilarated by the sheer joy on his face as he talked about the sport that had captured his heart, Julie felt her own heart beat a frantic melody. She could almost feel the wind on her face, the air lifting her up.

"And there's this moment of pure bliss when you wonder if maybe, just maybe, you'll never come back to earth," he said.

His blue eyes were lit from within, drawing her forward as if as she could hitch a ride on the wonder in his voice.

"You're skyrocketing through the air, the sky over you clear and bright and the white ground below. And there's this weightless sensation unlike anything else you've ever experienced. Like you could float forever and not miss having your skis touch down."

"You make it sound so breathlessly exciting," she murmured.

"Then the landing track rushes at you and there's a second right before touchdown that makes your heart leap in your throat. Will you stick it? Will you bobble and tumble and crash? The not knowing..." He took a deep breath through his nose and exhaled through his mouth. "Addictive."

She sat back, feeling as though she'd run a mile uphill.

Addictive. Spoken like a true adrenaline junkie.

If she'd needed a reminder why she shouldn't get involved with this man, he'd just delivered one. She dropped her gaze to her plate and wondered why she felt so dejected.

Nick watched the play of emotions over Jules's expressive face. She'd been caught up in what he was saying; he'd seen the way her eyes had flared, the pulse point at the base of her neck jumping and her lips parting as she sat on the edge of her seat. Then all of a sudden she'd deflated, like a balloon losing air. She poked at her salad, her eyes downcast, her mouth pinched at the corners.

"Okay, what's wrong?" he asked.

She shook her head, visibly pulled herself

together and lifted her chin. "Nothing. Can you tell me about your training? I've heard you ski off ramps into large pools."

"We do and I would love to tell you all about it. But first I want you to tell me why you look like I just kicked your puppy."

She laughed and waved her fork dismissively. "Nonsense. I don't know what you mean."

He arched an eyebrow. "Come on, Jules, spill it."

"I think it's great that you get so much pleasure from jumping. You're very good at it."

He wasn't going to let her get away with that. He reached out and placed his hand over hers. "Did I say something to upset you?"

"No, no." She gave a vigorous shake of her head. "It's not you. It's me."

"That sounds like something one would say when breaking up with someone. Are you breaking up with me already? On our first date?"

"Don't be ridiculous. We're not dating."

"I'm teasing you." He wished she'd worn her hair in a braid so he could tweak it. He was acutely aware they weren't dating. Reporter, remember? Except this was Julie. He had a hard time putting her in the same category as any other reporter. "Now, tell me what upset you."

"You're not going to let this go, are you?"

"Nope."

She took a drink of lemonade and set her glass down. "I was engaged two years ago to a guy who...had an addictive personality."

Why did he feel as though he'd misjudged a landing? "Were engaged? Meaning you aren't now?"

"I broke it off."

"Was he a gambler?" A logical assumption about a person with an addictive personality.

Her mouth pulled up at one corner. "I wouldn't be surprised, but not that I know of. He liked to say he lived life to the extreme. He was an adrenaline junkie. Into fast cars, fast motorbikes, fast boats. Rock climbing, BASE jumping, skydiving."

"And that didn't appeal to you." It wasn't a question but a statement. She was the type of woman who'd appreciate fine art, quiet sunsets and classical music. He couldn't see her willingly leaping out of a plane or off a building. Her hands were too delicate for the rough business of rock climbing. And she probably drove sedately, always just under the speed limit.

"The opposite."

All his assumptions crumbled with those two words. "Really? So you'd go skydiving or rock climbing?"

"I did." She wrinkled up her nose in a cute way that made him smile. "I'm not strong enough for the rock climbing." A smile lit up her eyes. "But I enjoyed the skydiving."

"I'd have never guessed you had that in you."

She shrugged. "You don't know me. So how would you know what I like?"

She had a point. Just because they'd grown up in the same town, in the same radius of life, didn't mean they knew anything about each other. Yet he felt a connection to her in a way he hadn't with anyone else. Ever. A very unnerving realization. "Then why'd you break it off?"

"Unfortunately, fast women were on his list, too...." Her voice trailed off and her gaze dropped to her plate.

"You being the exception, of course," Nick pointed out.

She shrugged again.

The guy must have been wrong in the head to blow a chance with a quality woman like Julie. Not that Nick wanted a chance with her. He couldn't forget her ambitions.

Suddenly long, hairy legs appeared over

the top of her shoulder, then the body of a gnarly spider came into view. A two-by-two-inch dark brown spot against the creamy off-white of her sweater. Nick sucked in a breath. His heart pounded as though he'd taken a spin down a double black diamond run. "Julie, don't move."

"What? Why?"

He picked up a butter knife from the table.

Her eyes widened. "Uh, Nick, your arm."

He followed her gaze to an exact twin to the spider on her shoulder. All his childhood nightmares came rushing back in vivid images.

"That's a hobo spider," she whispered. "Their bite can be deadly."

# FIVE

*"Aaaack!"* Nick yelled, flinging the spider off his arm.

Julie would have found Nick's reaction amusing if she hadn't felt the tickle on the side of her neck letting her know there was a spider crawling on her, as well.

"Uh, Nick," she squeaked. "A little help here."

Nick thrust the knife toward her and with a quick flip of his wrist, he tucked the knife under the spider on her shoulder and flung it away. He jumped to his feet and held out his hand to her. "I hate spiders."

Shuddering, Julie grabbed his hand and scrambled off the bench. She did the heebie-jeebies dance, her skin tightening with revulsion. "Are there any more?"

"I hope not."

Her gaze on landed the spider crawling up his thigh.

"Another one," she screeched, pointing.

Nick let loose a roar of disgust. Scooping up the butter knife again, he scraped the arachnid off, flinging the offending creature toward the back of the trailer.

The motor home door jerked open and Ted stormed in with his gun drawn. "Mr. Walsh?"

"Spiders!" Nick grabbed Julie's hand and headed toward the exit. "Out. We need to get out."

Confusion played on Ted's face, but he retreated, allowing Nick and Julie to stumble out of the RV. Once they hit the ground they both did the heebie-jeebies dance. Julie met his wild-eyed gaze.

A grin suddenly broke out on his handsome face.

Nick planted a hand on the side of the vehicle and bent over with laughter.

Julie giggled and couldn't stop stomping her feet in time with the shivers still coursing through her.

Ted put away his weapon and folded his arms over his chest. "What is going on?"

Straightening, Nick rocked back on the heels of his leather boots. "Hobo spiders. Three of them. Big, hairy and ugly."

A fresh wave of revulsion gushed over

her, causing more shudders. "Their venom is nasty. I've seen pictures of bites. The skin and tissue surrounding the area of contact harden and die. And if not treated quickly…"

Ted's frown deepened. He stepped a few feet away and made a phone call.

Nick groaned. "Gee, thanks for that image."

More giggles bubbled up. "The famous athlete who risks life and limb by doing incredibly challenging flips and twists high in the air has an Achilles' heel," Julie teased.

"Yeah, you got me." He made a face of distaste. "You were just as freaked out."

"I'm a girl. I'm allowed to be freaked out."

He scoffed. "You're going to play the gender card?"

"If the gender fits…"

"I'll have you know I'm secure enough in my manhood to admit there are two things in this world that will make me scream like a little girl—spiders and snakes."

"Phobias, huh?"

"Big time. Remember the fifth-grade science fair?" Nick asked.

"Vaguely. I think I did something on photosynthesis."

"Mine was on rockets."

She laughed as a vision of him launching himself into the sky appeared in her mind. "Figures."

"Robbie Blake did his on spiders." Nick pulled a face of disgust.

"Oh, yeah, I remember. He brought those fake, rubbery ones to school. He stuck one in my desk."

"He stuck one down my shirt."

She snickered. "But you knew it was fake, right?"

"Yes. But wait, the story gets better," he said. "Three nights later I woke in the middle of the night and found a spider crawling across my chest."

"Ick, how awful."

"Freaked me out. I had nightmares for months after. And I know it was a black widow, though my dad says it was a regular house spider, but I saw the orange hourglass on its belly before I ran screaming to my parents' room."

The image of the kid he'd been tearing out of bed, screaming for his mommy, had her grinning. "Okay, I can understand your phobia of spiders. Why snakes?"

His top lip curled. "Summer camping trip to the Sierra Nevada Mountains in California when I was twelve. Came face-to-face with a rattler. I thought for sure I was a goner."

"That would be terrifying. But it didn't strike?"

"No. My dad chopped its head off with a shovel."

"Ew. Gross."

Nick's chuckle rumbled from his chest. "Exactly. We skinned it and ate the meat."

Her stomach heaved. "That's even more gross."

He grinned, clearly enjoying her freaked-out state. "I made a key chain out of the rattle. I had it for years, until it fell apart."

Ted came back. "The police and an exterminator are on their way."

Nick's laughter died. His jaw visibly tightened. "Police?"

The grim set to Ted's mouth made Julie's tummy tumble. "Poisonous spiders in your trailer? One, maybe, but three?" He shook his head. "No way. The exterminator said they are aggressive when threatened. We need to stay out of the motor home."

The implications ran through Julie like a freight train. "You think the spiders are another attempt on Nick's life?"

"It can't be," Nick said. "No one could orchestrate a spider bite."

"Maybe not with one spider, but with multiple…"

Ted's grim expression left no doubt that he thought someone had deliberately placed the spiders in the motor home in an attempt to hurt Nick.

"No one but you, me, Frank, Lee and Gordon has had access to the motor home."

"The grocery delivery guy," Ted stated.

"You checked the groceries," Nick said. "And we were there with him."

"I'm not saying I know how he smuggled them in," Ted said. "Or how they got on you."

"But why would some random guy want to hurt Nick?" Julie asked.

"Maybe he has a grudge against Nick. Or someone could have paid him." Ted shrugged. "We won't know until the police have him in custody and ask."

Nick swiped a hand over his jaw. "Sorry, Julie. This is such a mess."

"It's not your fault," she assured him.

But it was. Nick hated that she'd been put in danger because of him. So had his friends. "We'll have to reschedule."

"We can do that. Maybe tomorrow after church?"

A car pulled up, drawing Nick's attention. A short, round man climbed out of the sedan.

Detective Agee. The man reminded Nick of a Weeble. The musical rhyme from his childhood toy played in his head.

Agee stuck out his hand. "Mr. Walsh, I understand there's been some more trouble."

"You could say that," Nick replied, shaking his hand. The detective had been the one to respond after the threatening note had arrived. "We're not sure what to make of it."

Agee turned to Ted. "You're Ted Gavin?"

"Yes, sir." Ted shook his hand. "We spoke on the phone."

"You said something about spiders?"

While Ted explained the situation, Nick turned to Julie. "Hanging around me isn't a good idea."

"You're not getting out of the interview that easily," she stated. Determination shone in her bright blue eyes.

"I would hate for you to get hurt because of me."

"My choice."

Another car came to a screeching halt and Gordon jumped out. "Nick, are you okay? Ted called and said there was another attempt on your life. This is so insane."

Nick held up a hand. "I'm fine. The police are here and Ted's got everything under control." He spent the next ten minute calming his manager down.

"Here's the exterminator," Julie said gesturing to the blue-and-white van pulling in behind the RV.

A tall man in a blue jumper got out and sauntered over. "I'm Allan. I hear you have a spider issue?"

"We found three hobo spiders inside," Nick said, directing him to the front door.

"Now that's a bit strange." Allan eyed the motor home. "I'll take a look and lay out some traps."

"Can't you fumigate?" Gordon asked.

"I can if you want. Not sure it will do the trick. It will probably only kill the good spiders," the man said.

"There are good spiders?" Nick asked, making a face.

The guy laughed. "I'll spray and set traps. May take a few days before the RV is livable."

"I'm staying at a hotel," Nick said.

"It may be difficult to find anything with the festival in full swing," Julie commented. "What about your parents?"

Nick's gut clenched. "The memorial service is in a few days. I don't want to burden them with this."

Julie tucked in her chin. "They wouldn't

see it as a burden. They'd be concerned and want to do what they could to help."

Of course, she was right. Guilt and shame nibbled at his conscience. The last time he'd seen his mother, she'd been grief stricken and angry. At him for not protecting Cody, and at God for taking Cody.

Nick was angry, too. At himself. He should have done a better job of watching out for his brother. "I'll call them if we can't find anything else." He wasn't ready to face Mom yet.

Gordon took out his phone. "I'll see what I can find in the way of accommodations."

The exterminator gathered his supplies from the van and went inside the motor home.

"How about we walk up to the lodge for coffee?" Nick asked Julie, noticing how the winter sun hit her hair just right. In the ray of light focused on her, her hair appeared to be filled with tiny diamonds.

"Sure," she answered. "Bob should be here soon. We can shoot some footage of you at the training center."

"Mr. Walsh, I suggest you lie low," Ted said as he and Detective Agee walked over.

"It's bad enough I have to move out of my house on wheels, I'm not going to hide like some lizard under a rock," Nick groused. "You'll have my back."

Detective Agee lifted his hand. "Hold up, Mr. Walsh. In light of the ambulance incident last night, I put a rush in for the crime scene techs to look at your ski. It was definitely tampered with."

Nick's mouth went dry. Whoever had tampered with his ski had done so before Nick arrived in Bend. The skis hadn't left his or his team's sight since they'd arrived in town. He couldn't say the same for when they were in Whistler or Copper Mountain, the sites of his last two competitions.

Agee flipped open his notebook. "Three incidents within twenty-four hours of each other. Who wants you dead, Mr. Walsh?"

Anger churned in the pit of Nick's gut. He'd been asking himself that same question for months. "I don't know. If I did, I'd tell you."

"There was another attempt," Gordon said, closing his phone.

Agee turned his attention to Gordon. "Fill me in on what happened."

"This past November, after the U.S. Grand Prix in Sun Valley, Idaho, someone cut the brake line on Nick's rental." Gordon wiped a hand over his face. "He could have died."

Nick met Julie's concerned gaze. Though she didn't show it, she must be thrilled to have so much fodder for her story.

"I'd taken the national title hours before and wanted a little time alone." As he always did after a competition. Driving helped to calm him, ground him after the adrenaline rush of competing. "I'd taken off in the SUV, not really knowing where I was headed, and found myself on a lonely mountain road winding around Bald Mountain."

The scenery had been breathtaking. "A deer ran out in front of me. I slammed on the brakes. For a moment, the brakes held, the truck slowed." His gut clenched with the memory. "I heard a snap and no longer had brakes."

He blew out a breath as the memory tightened his chest. "The vehicle skidded off the road and down an embankment, colliding with a tree. I walked away with a minor cut on my forehead and some burns from the air bag."

"Nick, that's terrible," Julie said.

"And the police investigation?" Agee jotted notes on a pad with a chewed-up pencil.

"Nothing," Gordon bit out. "Whoever did it was careful. Left no evidence."

"I'll contact the lead on the case and follow up," Agee promised.

Nick blew out a frustrated breath. "There is someone you should talk to. Katherine Rogers. She goes by Kitty. She was present both times something happened."

Gordon stared at him. "You know, you're right. She was in Idaho when you had your car accident. She's here now."

"Why would Kitty want to hurt you?" Julie asked.

Nick turned to her and noticed for the first time her cameraman, Bob, had arrived. The big black camera was up and aimed at Nick.

Trying to keep his irritation from flaring out of control, Nick shot Julie a sharp look. "Can you let me know when you're taping before the fact?"

Julie grimaced and put her hand over the lens. "Sorry."

Bob lowered the camera. The dude stared Nick down. "Not her fault, man."

Nick acknowledged Bob's statement with a tip of his chin.

"Hey, are we having a party?" Frank asked as he and Lee joined them.

Gordon explained to the guys what had happened.

Lee shuddered. "That's sick, man. Who'd do that?"

Frank sidled up close to Julie, drawing Nick's gaze.

"So you're doing a feature on Nick, huh?" Frank asked.

"Yes, I am." She smiled at him.

"He's not the only one vying for a spot on the team traveling to the games," Frank said. "Nick's not the only star in this circus. I've a good shot at it and so does Lee."

"So I've heard. I'd love to interview you both, as well."

"Anytime, anywhere." The suggestive tone in Frank's voice set Nick's teeth on edge.

"Come by the studio Monday at two," Julie replied briskly. She turned to Lee. "You, too."

"Sounds good," Lee said.

Unreasonable irritation washed through Nick. There was no good reason for him to feel the spurt of jealousy at his friend's flirting or that Julie would be interviewing Frank and Lee. They were both great skiers and good friends. And Nick had no claim on Julie. And wanted no claim on Julie. He blew out a breath and reined in the possessive feelings.

Nick moved to stand on the other side of Julie. "I didn't mean to snap at you earlier."

She angled away from Frank to put a hand on Nick's arm. "You're forgiven. If you'd rather we do the interview tomorrow or Monday, I'll understand."

"Yeah, that'd be good." Nick liked having her attention way more than he should. He noted the rueful twist of Frank's lips before he walked away.

"I need my purse and smart tablet," she said, looking at the RV.

Nick went to the door and cracked it open. Allan pushed it open the rest of the way and stood in the doorway. He held the baseball caps provided by Thunderbird in his glove-covered hands. "I discovered how the spiders got inside the motor home. I found two more tucked inside the sweatband of each hat."

Nick met Julie's stunned gaze. They'd had the hats on their heads. Revulsion trembled through Nick.

Agee stepped over. "Where did you get the hats?"

"They were sent by courier this morning from Thunderbird, my sponsor," Nick answered. Dumbfounded, he couldn't believe anyone at Thunderbird would want to do him harm.

"I'll track down the courier," Agee said. "I need the hats and the box they came in. Let me get an evidence bag from my car." He jogged away as Allan retreated back inside.

A moment later Allan appeared in the door-way with the hats tucked back into the box.

Agee returned with a large paper bag.

"Here you go," Allan said, slipping the box into the bag. "I've trapped five so far. The ones you flung will take longer to find."

"I'll take this to the crime scene techs. Hopefully, they can lift some forensics off them," Detective Agee said. "I'll let you know if I find out anything."

Nick shook Agee's hand. "Thank you."

Agee's eyebrows twitched. "Doing my job." And then he got in his car and drove away.

Before Allan disappeared inside again, Nick asked, "Hey, can you grab Julie's purse? And the tablet propped up behind the dining table?"

"Sure can." He came back a moment later. "Here you go. I checked the purse, and it's spider-free."

Nick handed Julie the bag and tablet. "I'm sure you got some good stuff here."

She half laughed, half grimaced. "Of us freaking out!"

"Right. That would make for a story."

"Any chance I'll see you at church tomorrow morning?" she asked.

He hesitated. Over the past year God had felt very distant. He wasn't sure how to recapture the closeness he'd enjoyed before Cody's death. "I can't promise I will."

Julie's shoulders drooped and her teeth tugged at her bottom lip. A gesture he remembered well from when they were kids. Usually right before a test. Not that she ever received any grade lower than an A-minus as far as he knew. She heaved a breath and straightened. "I hope that doesn't mean you've walked away from your faith?"

"No. Not walked away, but certainly drifted."

"Then it would be good for you to come to church. Same time as always."

Every Sunday growing up, Nick's family had moved around the nave, sometimes sitting in back, sometimes sitting up front, left side, right side. Mom always said she wanted to meet new people and the only way to do that was to find a new spot each week.

Did his mom still do that? Or was she still estranged from God, too? A welling tide of sorrow and pain rose. He hadn't talked to his mom since Cody's funeral, except for a few brief phone calls. He'd seen Dad once when he'd come to Lake Tahoe for the U.S. Aerial Freestyle World Cup. The sadness between them had made the weekend tense. Dad had said to give Mom more time. He wasn't sure how much time she'd need to forgive him. Or if she ever would.

Maybe attending good old Bend Community Church in the morning would bring him some peace. "I'll think about it," he said hoping to take away the fretfulness in Julie's pretty eyes.

Gordon stepped over. "I was telling the guys that all the hotels in town are booked. I did find a couple of places that would have rooms available tomorrow night. We'll have to drive over to Warm Springs and stay at the Kah-Nee-Ta Resort tonight."

"That's an hour and half away," Julie said. "Why not stay in Sunriver in one of the gated communities? My stepdad might have a place that you could rent for the duration of your stay."

"That's a good idea," Gordon said. "Can you call him?"

Julie glanced at Nick. He nodded his approval with a slight smile. Her heart did a little skip. She busied herself with the phone to combat the reaction she was having. The slightest smile made her heart pick up speed. She was acting like a teen again, pining for the most popular athlete in school.

*Get a grip and get over it.*

Marshal answered on the first ring. "Julie, is everything all right?"

She blinked. No greeting, just assuming

she wasn't okay. Annoyance crept into her tone. "Everything is fine. I have a question."

"And I will try to answer."

"It's more like a favor than a question," she said. Anxiety churned in her tummy. She rarely asked him for anything; she was afraid he'd think this was too much of an imposition. "Do you have any rental homes in one of the gated communities? Nick Walsh and his teammates need a place to stay."

"Let me see," he said. After a long moment of silence, Marshal returned to the phone. "I don't have anything available this week."

"Okay. It was worth a shot," she said with dread knotting her chest. She hated to disappoint Nick.

"Why don't you invite them all to our house?" Marshal asked.

Julie did a mental double take. "Really? You'd be okay with strangers coming to stay while you're in residence?" When he traveled he rented out his own house for a premium.

"If it brings you home for a few days, then yes," he said.

"Thank you," she said. "That's very generous."

"I'll call the gate and let them know to expect you and your friends."

Marshal hung up, leaving Julie a little

stunned. Marshal had not only offered to let Nick and his friends stay at the house, but he'd made it plain that Julie was to stay there, as well. He'd been trying to get her to move in with him since he and Mom had the house built ten years ago. He'd been putting more pressure on her lately. Seemed he was getting his wish. Temporarily.

"I have a solution to your problem," she told Nick and the guys. "My stepdad has invited you all to his house. It's big enough to accommodate all five of you." She refrained from saying she'd be joining them. "It's in a gated community with twenty-four-hour security patrolling the grounds. The house has a state-of-the-art alarm system."

"That sounds like the perfect setup," Ted commented.

Nick stroked his chin. "I wouldn't want to impose."

"You wouldn't be." She could see the internal debate in his expression. "Nick, if not for yourself, then for your teammates. One of them could have easily been bitten."

Her word had the desired result. He decided. "We'll accept your stepdad's generous offer."

Julie was glad to help, but the knot in her chest tightened even more. All this talk of attempted murder and knowing how much danger Nick was in only made asking Marshal for help that much more profound because she was putting Marshal and herself in potential danger, though she truly believed they would be safe at Marshal's house. Still, asking for help didn't come easily. She couldn't remember the last time she'd asked her stepdad for a favor. Or for anything, really. He had helped pay her college tuition, but she fully intended to pay it back one day. Her mother had instilled in her the need to stand on her own two feet.

Contemplating going to her condo and packing made her realize this couldn't have been a more perfect setup if she'd planned it herself. She'd have Nick and his buddies as a captive audience. They'd have to find the time to talk with her. She slanted a glance at Bob. She couldn't ask him to be at the house late at night or too early in the morning. No, she would be on her own, under the same roof as Nick, sharing the same air. Staying professionally detached was becoming harder by the minute.

# SIX

Julie stayed and they ended up spending the rest of the afternoon at the training center, which was part of the mountain's draw for many winter athletes. Nick put on his best behavior for the camera, though he couldn't help glancing over his shoulder every few minutes. The attempts on his life were wreaking havoc on his nerves. Gordon had gone to the pro shop and procured some Thunderbird apparel—sans spiders—for Nick and Julie to wear. With Bob filming and Ted keeping a discreet distance, Nick led Julie through the center, answering her questions, telling her, and the world, about learning to ski on Mt. Bachelor, how he'd become interested in aerials, and of his aspirations to compete with the world's best athletes.

"I was six when I found a jump someone had built on the trail. That was way before this mountain had a terrain park with ramps, rails and the works. I spent hours hurling myself off, trying to get as much air as possible. My ski coach caught sight of my attempts one day and suggested I take some gymnastic lessons during the summer. Mom stuck both me and Cody in classes. We loved jumping and flipping into the foam pit. I wasn't much for the bars or rings. But the vault was pretty cool, too."

"Your mom had her hands full with the two of you," Julie remarked good-naturedly.

"Yeah, she did. We were rambunctious and fought like crazy, but—" He had to look away as his throat closed with grief.

"You miss Cody."

Her softly spoken words impaled him. Understatement of the century. Remembering those carefree days with his brother brought an ache deep in his soul that he couldn't shake. An ache that reminded him to keep focused on the goal—winning gold for Cody.

He glanced at the camera, disliking that big black eye that stared at him with unrelenting intensity.

He'd been so distracted by how comfortable he felt with Julie and how easy talking with her was, he'd opened the door for conversation about Cody.

Ready to call a halt to this farce, Nick met Julie's blue gaze.

There was compassion in her eyes. But there was also a battle raging in her expression. He waited, his breath trapped in his lungs. Would she press him to talk about Cody?

Nick understood her desire to get her promotion, but he wouldn't drag Cody through the media mud. Not again.

"Is your first coach still here?" she finally asked.

Letting out a grateful breath, he acknowledged her kindness with a nod and a smile. "Coach Anderson retired a few years ago. But I bet there are lessons going on."

Julie's approving smile hit his chest like a ray of sunlight, radiating warmth through him. He pushed out the door of the center and welcomed the chilly air, needing to cool off. He had to get a grip. *Stay focused, dude.*

They found a teen group lesson in session. The kids were excited when he stepped up. For the next hour he answered questions and talked about skiing. The kids were especially interested in hearing about the upcoming games.

"Are you going?" one kid of about fourteen asked. "I saw you wipe out last night."

"Yeah, I biffed pretty bad, but I walked away. And that's a good day. Taking a tumble is part of the deal. You have to learn your limits and know when to bail."

"Will you get to hold the torch and light the flame?" a girl decked out in a red ski suit asked. Her light brown eyes were huge with curiosity.

"No, that honor is reserved for natives of the host country."

"So if the winter games were held in the U.S., you'd get to light the flame?" another girl asked.

Nick laughed. "If I were asked, I'd be honored."

"Okay, guys," the ski instructor interrupted, putting a halt to the questions. "We've got a mountain to tame. Let's get to it."

When the instructor led the kids to the ski lift, Nick wanted so badly to go with them. He was itching to feel the wind against his face, to zip down the hill as if he could outrun the world. Though the breathless feeling of jumping was exhilarating, he relished the downhill speed, as well.

"You were good with those kids."

Turning to face Julie, he smiled. "Someday I'd like to coach."

"You'd do well at it."

"Hey, Julie, the light's fading," Bob said. "Can we call it a wrap for today?"

"Yes, of course," Julie answered.

Nick checked his phone clock and was surprised to see how much time had passed. This hadn't been as bad as he'd anticipated.

They returned the clothing they'd borrowed for the show and then headed toward the parking lot. It had cleared out as the sun started its descent on the horizon, painting the sky in streaks of pink and orange.

Nick watched with interest as Bob touched Julie's elbow, pulling her to a halt. "You gonna be okay? I'm not sure about you taking these guys to your house."

Julie smiled at her coworker. "It's my stepdad's house, and it will be fine. I'll see you on Monday."

Bob scowled at Nick. "Be careful with her."

At face value the words could have meant anything, but Nick had a feeling he'd just been warned not to hurt Julie. Like he had any intention of doing so.

Obviously the man cared about Julie. Nick wondered just how deeply those feelings went and if Julie returned them.

"No worries, buddy. She's safe."

Bob grunted and headed in the opposite direction.

Two little frown lines appeared between Julie's eyes. "He's been acting strange all day."

"I wouldn't stress about it," Nick said, unable to keep the amusement from his tone. Obviously, she didn't realize Bob had a thing for her. Which had to mean she didn't have a thing for Bob. Now why did that bit of knowledge lift Nick's mood?

She gave him a confused look. "He's usually much more congenial than he was today."

Nick's phone chirped. He answered. Gordon wanted to know when and where to meet them so he and the guys could follow Julie to her house.

"We'll meet you in the parking lot in five," he said and hung up.

With Ted keeping pace with Nick on one side and Julie on the other, they headed out of the training center. Julie slipped slightly on the sloping walkway. Nick tucked her into his side to keep her upright. The shy, grateful smile she gave him sent his heart galloping. He ignored how good it felt to have her meld against him, as though they were a couple. He hadn't been part of a couple in longer than he cared to remember.

He didn't have time for a love life with his travel and training schedule. He barely had time for friends, let alone dating. Hanging out with his female teammates didn't count, since he regarded each one like a sister he'd never had. He certainly didn't view Julie with the same lens. He was skating on dangerous ice here. Remembering why he needed to keep a distance from her was proving difficult at every turn.

He liked her, and if his life wasn't so complicated and she wasn't a reporter, he might want to see where a relationship with her would go. But his life was complicated and commitment was a fire he wasn't ready to leap into, especially not with a woman who had an agenda that put his reputation and that of his brother on the line.

He had to remember someone was trying to kill him. He was waiting to hear if he'd be going to compete in the biggest sporting event in the world. And Julie was who she was. Or rather, what she was—a reporter, which put her in the frenemy category. Friend, yet enemy.

The gunning of an engine rent the air, grabbing Nick's attention. His gaze whipped to his left. A white utility van barreled down the aisle of the parking lot.

He and Julie stood directly in its path.

"Watch out!" Ted shouted while giving Nick a shove to move him out of the way.

Julie screamed.

Nick swung his arm out to capture Julie by the waist and, using the momentum of Ted's push, dove to the side, taking Julie with him. They landed hard between two parked cars. He tried to break their fall, taking the brunt of the impact himself. His heart beat like a stampede of mule deer.

The loud crack of a gun echoed in Nick's ears. Were they being shot at? He folded himself over Julie, protecting her as best he could against the unseen threat.

Nick's mind spun. Had the driver of the van simply not seen them or was this another deliberate attempt on his life?

"Are you guys all right?"

Ted's frantic question pierced through the thundering in Nick's ears. The resort parking lot came into focus. He rolled off Julie and sat up.

"Yeah." His voice came out ragged. "I think we are. Julie?"

She lay on her back staring up at the dusky sky, her face pale. She didn't respond.

Panic seized Nick's breath. "Jules?"

She gripped his hand and squeezed. "Give me a minute," she whispered.

The sound of pounding feet on the pavement sent a fresh wave of alarm through Nick. Ted whirled to face the oncoming threat, his weapon drawn.

"Whoa! Just us," Gordon said as he, Frank and Lee drew to a halt.

Ted lowered his weapon.

Nick looked up at him. "Did you shoot at the van?"

"Yep, took out his taillight. That will give the police something to look for, since it was a generic white van with no markings and the plates missing."

"What happened?" Gordon asked, his gruff voice quaking. "Nick, you okay? Tell me you didn't get hurt!"

"I'm fine." Ignoring the others squeezing close, Nick went to his knees and checked Julie for injuries. "Are you hurt?"

She pushed his hands away. "Just. Give. Me. A. Minute."

He lifted his hands. His pulse beat erratically.

Julie came up on her elbows. "That was close."

"Are you hurt?" Nick persisted, needing to know she was unharmed.

She shook her head. Strands of hair had broken free from her bun, making her look more like the girl he remembered. He smoothed a hand over her cheek. "That's a relief."

Her pretty blue eyes searched his face. "You?"

"A few scrapes and more bruises, but nothing that would keep me from competing." He shifted his attention to Ted. "Call the police."

"Already called it in," he replied.

Nick rose and held out his hand to Julie. She slipped her smaller hand into his. Her skin was soft and smooth, her bones delicate, yet her grip was strong. When she had her feet under her, he tried to let go of her hand.

She held on for a moment longer. "Thank you for saving my life."

Uncomfortable with her gratitude and the way her eyes looked at him with a bit of hero worship, he shrugged. "I was saving my own skin, as well."

A corner of her lush mouth lifted. "Yeah, well, thanks just the same."

"Did you get a look at the driver?" Frank asked.

Nick shook his head. "It happened too fast. The windows were tinted."

Lee clapped him on the back. "Glad you're okay. You're like a cat with nine lives, dude."

"Landing on my feet is my specialty," Nick quipped.

Lee grinned. "As well as saving damsels in jeopardy."

Nick barked out a short laugh. "And that."

"The police will be here shortly," Ted said. "Let's get back inside."

"Julie, you should probably leave. I don't want you getting hurt because of me," Nick said.

"Save your breath," she replied. "I'm staying. And you're coming with me to Marshal's. End of discussion. Okay?"

He cocked an eyebrow. "When did you get pushy?"

One side of her mouth tipped up. "About the time you popped back into my life."

He laughed, liking her spunk. He sent up a silent plea for her safety and hoped God would listen.

They waited inside the lodge, and by the time the police arrived, took their statements and left, night had fallen. After a quick dinner in the lodge restaurant, Julie gave Gordon her stepfather's address in case they got separated.

"You guys give us a ten-minute head start," Ted instructed. "I need to be sure we're not followed."

Acutely aware that Ted had his hand on his weapon in case of another attempt as he escorted them to Julie's car, Nick kept Julie close so he could grab her again if needed. He hated that she'd come close to being hurt twice now because of him. She led them to a red hybrid hatchback car with snow tires and shiny rims.

Nick let out a low whistle. "Sweet car."

She beamed. "Thanks. It handles amazingly well. But then again, it's an all-terrain vehicle."

"I should drive," Ted said as he stopped behind them. "You two sit in back. Less of a target that way."

Nick's heart thumped at the reminder of the danger plaguing him.

Julie's eyes widened. "That works for me." She held out the keys attached to a heart-shaped gold fob.

Nick placed his duffel bag into the trunk. He and the guys had removed their things from the motor home after the exterminator had inspected their clothing to make sure no hitchhiking spiders were trying to escape the RV.

Climbing into the backseat of the car next to Julie, Nick tried not to notice how nice she smelled or the way her knee brushed against his in the tight confines.

"I'm going to take the route through town

instead of the back roads in case that white van decides to come after you again," Ted told them.

As Ted drove them down the mountain to the valley floor below and into the town of Bend, Julie gave directions in between keeping up a continuous dialogue, telling Nick of the changes in town. He figured talkativeness was a response to the adrenaline of almost being mowed down.

"A new Thai restaurant that I haven't tried yet took over the space where Fischer's Bakery used to be," she said, pointing out the window.

"Too bad about the bakery. They had the best bear claws around," Nick remarked, remembering back to when he and Cody would ride their bikes into town and stop in to say hi to Irving Fischer. He'd always give them a free carton of chocolate milk to go with their pastries. "What happened to Mr. Fischer?"

"He retired and moved to Florida," Julie said. "He said the winters were getting to his bones."

"I can't imagine a nicer place to retire to than Bend," Nick stated. "The winters here are mild compared to the winters in Lake Placid or Deer Park, Utah."

"I've never been to either," she said. She

leaned forward to give Ted directions, leading them out of downtown toward the resort area a few miles outside of town. Sitting back, she said, "The whole community has embraced going green. Everyone's going organic and using local growers and solar power so they leave as little a carbon footprint as possible."

"There are places all across the country going green," Nick said. "The push to recycle and conserve resources is a good thing."

"I volunteer with the Upper Deschutes River Council helping to care for the Deschutes River. Once a year in June we have a cleanup day. It's actually a fun time as the community comes together to pick up trash and pull noxious weeds."

"Cody and I loved to white-water raft down the Deschutes. Do they still allow that?"

"Sure do," Julie said. "You should come home in the summer and go rafting."

He held her gaze and found himself drifting into the clear blue of her eyes. "If my training schedule allows time." He could easily make time, but coming home was painful with memories of Cody everywhere he looked.

"I'd like to hear about your training regime."

"It's rigorous and demanding, but I love

every second of it." And with his bruised arm keeping him off the slopes, he'd better hit a gym soon. He didn't want to lose his edge.

"Loving what you do is important."

"And you love being in front of the camera," he said. "You're very natural at it."

"Thank you. I didn't start out that way. I was a nervous mess the first few times I practiced, but Bob was patient and helped me."

Nick had no doubt Bob enjoyed helping Julie. The guy was at least ten years older than her and probably liked having a younger woman looking up to him. "Are you and Bob…"

"What?" She blinked at him. "Oh, no. We're friends. He's a good guy, though."

Recalling the way Bob had looked at her and acted all protective of her, Nick doubted the guy wanted to remain in the friend category. He didn't blame him. Julie was a great gal with a keen sense of humor and easy to get along with. She would be the type of girl he'd want to keep close if he was in a place in his life to have a relationship.

Well, except for her chosen profession. Or soon-to-be profession, he amended. He had no doubt she'd do well anchoring a segment on the televised lifestyle magazine *Northwest Edition.* She was engaging when she asked questions, making him feel as though they were friends chatting as they'd been doing in the car, instead of an interview. He was impressed with her.

However, he couldn't let his guard down around her. He couldn't control what she chose to say in front of the camera. And he was finding himself unable to control his emotions for her.

At some point she'd put her career ahead of his feelings. She would ask how he felt when Cody died, just as the reporters who'd camped outside the funeral had asked. Just like the reporters who crowded around him after every competition did. It didn't matter if he won or lost or placed, the reporters always reverted to the rumors surrounding Cody's death. The inane question of how he felt scraped across his nerves.

But it didn't matter how many times he corrected each and every newshound who stuck a microphone in his face demanding to know if Cody had been under the influence when he took that last jump, they didn't believe him. The smug, you-can't-fool-me look that seemed to be a universal expression among reporters made Nick's hands clench.

His chest expanded with the force of his

inhale. He slowly let it out, hoping to curb the simmering anger that wanted to bubble up.

No, he couldn't forget that Julie's promotion rested on how well she could exploit his family's tragedy.

# SEVEN

A guard sat in the gatehouse at the entrance to the subdivision where Julie's stepfather, Marshal, lived. Floodlights illuminated a beautiful waterfall feature next to the tall metal gate and high brick wall that surrounded the neighborhood. Impressed with the setup, Nick turned to Julie. "You weren't kidding when you said gated community. Someone would have to have rappelling gear to climb that wall."

"Security's a big deal for a lot of these people," she replied as she jumped out of the backseat. She went in to the guardhouse to talk to the guy. She returned a few moments later with passes for them. "That's Steve, and he gave me passes for all of you. That way you can get in and out when you need to. I told him to expect Gordon soon."

The guard opened the big black gate. They drove through and proceeded through the neighborhood. Marshal's house was on a back lot with the backyard butting up against a golf course.

Away from the lights of town, the sky seemed darker and the stars more brilliant. The air smelled of pine and freshness, like the first snow of the season when he and Cody were kids. They'd wake early, gear up and make first tracks. The memories made Nick's heart ache. He wished he could bottle up the scent and take it with him as a keepsake of happier times.

The front of Marshal's home was made of rock and cedar. He couldn't see how big the place was in the dark, but he had the distinct impression it was sprawling. Julie unlocked the eight-foot-tall front door and led the way inside. Low lights from wall sconces gleamed on the entryway's cherrywood floors.

"Come in." She walked into the house, leaving him and Ted to trail behind.

"Where's your stepdad?" Nick asked. The house appeared closed up for the night. Though there were no lamps turned on in the main part of the house, light coming through the floor-to-ceiling windows dominating the back wall lent enough illumination that he could tell the kitchen and living room were combined in a lodge-style great room. The soaring ceiling gave a sense of spacious luxury as he passed through the living room and followed Julie down a hall. She hit the light switch, turning on overhead canned lights, creating a soft yellow glow.

"He's at a festival event tonight, schmoozing."

"Schmoozing?"

"Yes. He's in real estate. It's good business to network. You never know when someone will decide to put a piece of property up for sale. We probably won't see him until Monday morning. He'll come in very late and leave before the sun's even up."

"Even on a Sunday?"

"Weekends are the busiest days in his business." She opened the door on the right. "Ted, this is the closest room to the front door, as you requested."

"Thank you, Julie." Ted moved past her to inspect the bedroom. Nick caught a glimpse of a bed covered in a light brown comforter.

"Nick, you'll be across the hall," she said, moving to open the door. "Do you think Lee and Frank will mind sharing a room?"

Nick snorted. "They'll be stoked to sleep on a real mattress after spending most of the season in the motor home."

She smiled. "Good. I'll put them and Gordon in the other wing with Marshal. Each of the rooms has an en-suite bathroom."

"Where's your room?"

Even in the dim light of the hall, he saw the blush working its way up her neck. She pointed to the last door at the end of the corridor. "That's my room when I stay here."

A knock at the front door had her brushing past him. He moved to follow her as Ted stepped in front of them. "Let me."

Julie halted. Nick bumped into her back, his hand reflexively curving around her waist for balance.

Ted strode away to answer the door.

Nick's hand lingered. "Sorry about that."

She turned to face him. "No worries."

The light overhead hit her hair, making the strands shine. He noticed the cute sprinkle of freckles across the bridge of her nose. His gaze landed on her parted lips, and his breathing hitched as longing tugged at him. Slowly he raised his gaze to meet hers. Awareness shimmered in the air like an electric current. The urge to pull her close gripped him in a tight vise.

Voices coming from the entryway shattered the moment.

Nick stepped back.

Shaken by the strong allure of attraction, he ran a hand through his hair.

Julie's top teeth tugged at her bottom lip as uncertainty clouded her eyes.

"You'd better show the guys to their rooms."

She nodded and quickly retreated, disappearing toward the front of the house.

Slowly he followed, chiding himself for the momentary lapse in judgment. The last thing he needed to do was muddle the situation with Julie by giving in to his attraction to her. He had no intentions of finding himself in a romance. He wasn't ready for that kind of commitment. Especially not with the beautiful Julie, because she had the power to hurt him, to hurt his family. He had to stay cautious and keep an emotional barrier between them.

He hung back as Julie showed first Gordon to his room and then Frank and Lee to the room they would share. Two double beds were decked out in matching gray checked comforters. A plasma television and gaming system hung on the wall opposite the bed. The room looked like a teenage boy's room.

Frank dropped his duffel bag at the foot of the closest double bed. "Same old, same old. Stuck with you again."

Lee set his bag on the double bed closest to the window. "Dude, don't be a jerk. It beats a hotel."

"Yeah, but we have to share while the star gets his own room."

"Our day will come," Lee said quietly.

Frank snorted. "Yeah, maybe sooner rather than later."

Nick frowned. Where was this resentment coming from? He stepped into the doorway next to Julie. He met her curious gaze and shrugged. "Frank, buddy, I'll share with Lee. You take the single room."

Frank jerked around to face Nick. For a moment he looked tempted, then he shook his head. "Naw, man. That's okay. Besides, Nick, you need your beauty sleep."

"There's a pullout couch in the study if you'd prefer, Frank," Julie offered.

He waved her off. "I'm good. I've got earplugs."

"What's that supposed to mean?" Lee groused.

"You snore, dude," Frank stated, then looked to Nick for confirmation. "Right?"

Nick grinned. "Like a freight train."

Lee grabbed his chest and staggered back in mock pain. "You wound me."

Nick snorted. "Frank, you're a drama queen."

"Takes one to know one," he shot back with a grin.

Lee laughed. "I'm surrounded by divas."

"Hey, you'd better watch it," Frank grumbled and flopped back on the bed. "Ooh, nice and firm." He sat up and looked at Julie. "In all seriousness, thank you for hosting us."

Julie inclined her head. "You're welcome. And good night."

She walked back to the kitchen.

Nick followed. Ted closed his phone and walked into the living room to inspect the sliding glass door.

Nick noted the well-appointed kitchen and expensive granite. "This is a nice place. Big for only your stepdad to live here."

"Marshal has family from his first marriage," she explained. "His eldest son has two teenage boys who share that room when they visit."

"Where do they live?" Nick asked as they headed back toward Nick's room. Ted stayed a few paces behind them.

"Canada. His ex-wife moved there after their divorce. When Marshal married my mom, she insisted they have enough room for his other kids and their families during holidays. They've only come for a few visits that I'm aware of."

"That's too bad," Nick said. "It must be hard on Marshal."

Julie picked at her thumbnail for a moment, then tilted her head. "Yes. I think it is. He goes up there occasionally to see his grandkids."

"Do you get along with your stepsiblings?"

She leaned against the door frame while Ted disappeared into his room.

"I've only seen them a handful of times," she said. "They were much older than me when my mom married Marshal. And they weren't happy that he was remarrying."

"That must have been hard on you."

"I was used to being alone, so whether they wanted to see me or not didn't really make much difference."

"What happened to your father?"

She pushed away from the door frame and walked into the bedroom, flipping on the light. "He was killed in action in Desert Storm."

Sympathy curled a fist in Nick's gut as he joined her in the room. "I'm sorry. I didn't know."

"I didn't know him. I was only three when he died." She moved to the window and closed the curtains.

The room was large with light brown,

plush-looking carpet and walls that matched. A queen-size sleigh bed covered in muted blues and reds sat opposite a forty-inch plasma screen. An armoire stood in the corner beside a tall window covered by a patterned curtain matching the bedcoverings.

"Nice digs," he said as he set his duffel on the floor in front of the cedar chest at the foot of the bed.

She lingered by the door, looking as if she had something she wanted to say.

"Is something the matter?" he asked.

"I was hoping you'd change your mind about coming to church with me in the morning."

He inhaled as he turned the question over in his mind. He had contemplated attending, but that was before it was clear whoever wanted him dead had followed him home. Now he wasn't sure it would be safe. For himself and especially for everyone else. He was sure God would understand if he missed the service. He exhaled. "No. I'm not going."

Disappointment flickered in her eyes.

Compelled to reassure her he hadn't abandoned his faith, he added, "I'd like to, but it wouldn't be safe. I need to lie low."

"Right. It's too bad, though. I'm sure everyone would like to see you. Your parents usually attend."

Longing welled up. He missed his parents, but wasn't sure of the reception he'd receive. It was good to know Mom still went to church. "I'll see them on Thursday. It will be the one-year anniversary of Cody's death." His heart contracted painfully in his chest. Guilt ate at him.

Compassion softened her expression. "I'm sorry."

"There's a memorial service at the church. You're welcome to come."

"Thank you. Your parents will be grateful to have you there. It will mean a lot to them."

Emptiness settled in the pit of his stomach. "I'm not so sure."

Her eyebrows drew together. "Why do you say that?"

He swallowed as the need to talk bubbled up. But could he trust her not to use his pain to further her career? "I'm punchy. Don't listen to a word I say."

She crossed her arms over her chest. "Why do you think your parents wouldn't be happy to see you?"

Scrubbing a hand over his face, he took a seat on the chest at the foot of the bed. "Off the record?"

For a moment she was still and quiet, then she heaved a sigh and nodded. "Yes. Off the record."

He forced the words out. "Because I'm responsible for Cody's death."

Her arms fell to her side. She looked him hard in the eyes. "So you're saying you gave your brother drugs?"

"What?" Outrage at the suggestion choked him. He figured it was only a matter of time before she brought that up.

"Nick, you know as well as I do the top trending theory for Cody's death is drug usage. Witnesses claimed to have seen him taking something suspicious and acting as if he was under the influence."

"The internet is wrong. The witnesses are wrong. The autopsy showed no evidence of illegal drugs. He was exhausted, not high. We both were. We'd been training hard and competing even harder." Guilt tugged the truth from him. "I shouldn't have let him take that last jump. If I had stopped him, he'd be here."

"You can't know that."

Memories of that day rushed in, making his chest twist with pain. "I'd been working on a new trick, pushing the limit and doing okay. My landings needed work, but I was physically wiped. That had been happening a lot lately. After my last jump, I decided to call it quits for the day. But Cody wouldn't." Nick met her gaze. "He tried to do the same trick. It was out of his reach."

She winced. "He crashed."

Nick swallowed back the bile rising up at the memory. "He didn't make a full rotation and came down on his head. Broke—" Nick's voice caught. He had to clear his throat before he could continue. "Broke his neck. The doctors said he died instantly."

Julie moved to sit beside him. Taking his hand, she said, "Cody's death was not your fault. He chose to try something risky. You can't blame yourself for that."

"But I do. If I hadn't been showing off by doing the trick, then he wouldn't have felt like he needed to try it. Cody had grown increasingly cocky as the day wore on. A sign the fatigue was affecting him. He was always trying to one-up me."

He shook his head with self-loathing. "If I had made him stop…"

"That's a lot of *if*s," she said.

"Yeah, if only I had done something different."

"But Nick, life doesn't work that way."

He blew out a breath. "No, it doesn't." His fingers curled around hers. "I don't understand why he had to die." He turned to stare at her as the words he'd held in for so long came tumbling out. "Why did God let him die?"

As the words left his mouth, an anger he hadn't realized he harbored surfaced, bubbling up and erupting like a geyser in his soul. He wanted to roar with rage at God for letting his baby brother die. He wanted to weep with the grief engulfing him. He hung his head and squeezed his eyes tight.

"Oh, Nick. God didn't do this. Accidents happen. It's a part of the human condition. We're frail beings. Your brother made a risky choice. It wasn't your fault."

The tears he'd been unable to shed leaked from the corners of his eyes. He shook his head, denying her words, yet he knew what she said was true. God didn't orchestrate accidents. Cody had made a choice to take that jump in a desire to be like his older brother. No, God wasn't to blame. Only Nick.

Anguish for Nick settled in Julie's chest like a physical ache. He'd taken on the burden of guilt for the random accident that had caused his brother's death. It wasn't right for him to feel so guilty, yet she didn't know how to help.

She slid her arms around him and held him, hoping to offer some comfort. He remained stiff and unyielding. She pulled back to look into his eyes. His inscrutable gaze stared back, leaving her cold.

After a long moment, he said, "It's late. You should go to your room."

The rejection stung, though why she couldn't fathom. It wasn't as if she was pinning her heart on him. She let her arms fall away from him and stood. Despite her best intentions to shake off the prick of refusal, everything inside of her threatened to disintegrate into a puddle at his feet. Wrapping her arms around her middle, she stiffened her spine and plastered on a tight smile. "I hope you'll change your mind about church in the morning."

She turned and fled, closing the door to her room and leaning against the wood. Her heart raced and her mind brimmed with jumbled thoughts.

Nick Walsh was right down the hall.

He'd needed a safe place to stay. Concern for his safety had prompted the offer. It was a good solution. For him. But not so much for her.

Not only because of the danger looming over him like a dark cloud.

But because of the attraction she was fighting.

She should have left for her own home as

soon as she'd settled them all in their rooms, but she'd wanted to know more about Nick, wanted to ask about church and make sure he knew he'd be welcomed.

She hadn't counted on seeing his tears. Or having him push away her offer of comfort. And she sure hadn't figured on hurting, for him or because of him.

The last thing she wanted was to be attracted to him. Nick was not the type of guy she needed in her life. His life was transient, traveling from one competition to another, or spent at one of several training centers during the off-seasons. He wasn't the kind to settle down, to build a life in the place where they'd grown up. She couldn't imagine living anywhere but Bend. She'd known even in grade school that Nick was destined to leave. He'd always talked about seeing the world. And skiing had been his ticket to fulfill that dream.

No, when the time came and she was ready to put her heart out there again, it wouldn't be with a hotshot skier.

She wanted stable and steady. The kind of guy she'd never have to worry wouldn't return unscathed from some adventure or who would cheat on her just for the thrill of it. Someone whom she could always count on to be there for her. Someone who wouldn't push the limits to the extremes.

She had to keep Nick in perspective.

He was an old acquaintance who needed her support and could help her land her dream job in the process. Nothing more than that.

Nick tossed and turned, his mind replaying the moment when he'd tried to do the right thing by calling a halt to whatever was happening between him and Julie before the embers of attraction burst into flames. He'd hurt her. He'd seen it in her eyes, in the pinched lines around her mouth.

It was better this way, he rationalized. Better for them both to keep their relationship purely platonic. A working relationship. Except he was staying in her stepfather's home as a guest with her down the hall. At the time, it had seemed like the only choice to keep himself and his teammates safe.

But now…more than his life was at risk.

Friends. They could be friends. Except… except she'd basically said she believed all the gossip about Cody despite no proof or his word that the rumors weren't true.

In a moment of weakness, he'd let down his guard. He couldn't do that again.

A noise broke the silence of the shadowed room.

He sat up. Straining, he listened. The hairs on his arms rose and a shiver of unease slid down his neck. He climbed from the bed and made his way to double-check the window. The latch was turned. Still locked. Nick peered into the darkness beyond the windowpane. Through the glow of the moon, he could see the outline of patio furniture and some sort of rock sculpture in the backyard. Trees crusted with ice swayed.

Wind. He'd only heard the wind. He rolled his shoulders and forced himself to relax.

Now that he was up, he was thirsty. He left his room and made his way toward the kitchen. The refrigerator door's light glowed bright, giving off enough illumination for him to find a glass in the cupboard.

The tingling sensation in his fingers as he gripped the cup sent an alert signal jolting through him; tingling in his extremities was a sign his vitamin stores had dropped. He winced, remembering he hadn't taken his vitamin pack this morning. Part of his daily regimen was drinking a powdered mix of vitamins and minerals, with an extra dose of the B's. He could only blame his forgetfulness on the near-death experiences of the day.

Thankfully, he had vitamins in his luggage. He filled his cup from the refrigerator door. He had taken two steps when a whisper of movement froze him in place.

His heart hammered at his ribs.

Had the noise he heard earlier been an intruder? Had someone breached the safety of the house?

Caution pimpled his skin like moguls on a mountain. His frantic gaze searched the darkness for an enemy.

For a weapon.

# EIGHT

Sudden light filled the kitchen.

Blinking against the assault to his eyes, Nick's gaze zeroed in on Julie and the blood rushed to his head. He planted his feet wide as the momentary adrenaline blast ebbed, slowly draining into the floor. Not an intruder.

Putting a hand over her heart, Julie let out a noisy exhale. Beneath her Scottie dog–printed red flannel pj's, her shoulders were hiked to her ears, and the expression on her face reminded him of a rabbit caught in the garden. She looked ready to bolt. He'd felt the same just moments before.

"Sorry," Nick said, keeping his voice low. "I didn't mean to wake you."

Visibly shaking off her fright, she moved to the cupboard. "You didn't. I've been up for a while."

"Bad dreams?"

Taking out a mug, she shook her head. "Too keyed up. You?"

"I was thirsty." He held up the glass of water in his hand.

"Would you like some hot tea?"

"Water's good."

She filled the mug with water from the insta-hot plumbed into the sink and dropped a chamomile tea bag into the steaming liquid. She moved into the living room and flipped on the gas fireplace. An orange-and-gold flame danced in the hearth. Nick turned off the kitchen light and joined her on the over-stuffed leather couch. He stretched out his long legs and made himself comfortable. A decorative pillow separated them.

Aware of his close proximity and the musky smell of him, Julie grabbed an afghan from the back of the couch and spread it over herself like a shield against the force of his magnetism. He shouldn't look so good with his dark hair all bed mussed and his jaw unshaven. He had on sweat bottoms and a T-shirt that stretched across well-defined chest muscles. The bruise on his left arm was already starting to change from the deep purple to the slightly greenish hue of healing.

She sipped from her tea and concentrated on the dancing flames.

After a silent moment, Nick said, "This is nice."

She glanced at him, wondering what he meant. She decided to take his words at face value. "Yes, it is. The house is great. My mom was happy here."

"It's not often I get to kick back and just be," he said.

"Be?"

"Yeah. Most of the time I'm traveling in the motor home with the guys or staying in hotels. It's nice to be in a real home. It's nice to be here with you."

Not sure how to feel about the last part of his comment, especially after the way he'd rebuffed her earlier, she said, "Don't you have a home base?"

"I have a condo in Lake Placid near the training center. But I'm there less than half the year. The rest of the time I'm traveling."

"That must get tiring. I can't imagine sleeping in a motor home for days on end or staying in strange hotels night after night."

"Yeah, this lifestyle can be brutal at times."

"But you love it, right?"

"I don't know if *love* is the right word. It was exciting at first. But I'm getting on the old side of this sport."

She snorted. "Right, like twenty-six is old."

"It is in aerials. I'm the oldest on the team. And the young bloods are waiting for me to retire so they can move up."

"The competition doesn't end on the slopes then."

"No, it doesn't."

Julie thought of the line of helmeted, goggled competitors watching intently during the competition. The threatening note he'd talked about that had said TIME TO DIE.

"Could the reason someone is trying to kill you be to hurry along your retirement?"

"Detective Agee asked me the same thing. And, no, I can't believe that anyone on the team would resort to murder to get ahead."

"You never know what anyone is capable of."

"I suppose. But we're a tight group. I'd know if one of them wanted me dead."

"Maybe, maybe not. Is there anyone on the team who you don't get along with? Any sort of contention among your teammates? Even jokingly? Sometimes what we think is in jest can hide maliciousness." She remembered the way Frank had acted earlier. She hated to think he'd have anything to do with the threat against Nick.

He stared into the fire for a moment, then shook his head. "Not that I can think of."

"How well do you know Lee and Frank?"

His gaze snapped to her. "Well. They aren't just competitors. Not even just teammates. They're like brothers to me and Cody." His gaze dropped as he said his brother's name.

"I didn't mean to upset you."

He visibly shook off the grief and smiled at her. "You know, you'd make a good detective."

She laughed. "Asking questions is how I hope to make my livelihood."

"True. I don't remember you being so inquisitive."

"I was always inquisitive, just too shy to ask."

"You grew out of that."

"Maturity and practice."

"How did you end up working for a television lifestyle magazine?"

"It was a God thing." She slanted him a glance to see how he'd react to her statement.

"How do you mean?"

Maybe if he heard her story, he'd be more willing to cooperate. "I was finishing up my sophomore year of college and needed to decide which direction to take my learning in. One of my advisors, a dear Christian man who I respected a great deal, called me to his office and said he knew of a paid internship that he thought I'd be perfect for. At a television station as a production assistant's assistant. Professor Lemeke said he knew I was struggling to find where I belonged and that he had been praying for me. He said he had a strong feeling this was the path God had for me. I was skeptical. I couldn't see myself working in the television industry but felt like I should at least go to the interview he'd set up out of respect."

"The interview must have gone well."

"It did. I liked the production manager and the production assistant. And I was taken with the energy of the station and the personalities. I jumped in and it was the best decision for me. I did find the place where I belonged. I thought maybe I'd work toward writing the copy for the news or something like that."

"So now you're on the cusp of a promotion to anchor a lifestyle television show. How did that happen?"

"Some would say by chance, but I believe God had His hand on me. I'd been working there for two years while studying broadcast journalism. One day the host of *Northwest Edition* got food poisoning and couldn't go on. The production staff was in a panic. They decided to rerun an old interview Gloria had done with a local business owner. But they needed someone to introduce the segment and explain that Gloria was ill. The production manager decided a warm body was better than nothing. Next thing I know I'm sitting in makeup. Then in Gloria's chair. All I had to do was read from the teleprompter."

"And you were a natural," Nick stated.

"No, not hardly. I was stiff and scared and stumbled a bit over the words. But it was the most exciting and fun thing I'd ever done. The production manager was pleased. But more importantly, the station owner was pleased. They hired a cohost not long after Gloria's incident so that they'd always have someone to be on air. But the experience sparked something in me. I took on-camera acting lessons in addition to my college work. And Bob has worked with me, helping me to become comfortable in front of the lens."

"Good for you."

"It could be." She turned to face him and tucked her feet beneath her. She needed to make him understand how important this promotion was to her. "For the longest time it was just my mom and me. We had to be independent. We had to learn to take care of ourselves. Then she met and married Marshal.

All of a sudden someone else was taking care of us."

"That must have been a huge blessing for your mother."

Unexpected tears flooded her eyes. "It was. They were good together. He was good to her. Real good." Grief stabbed at her. Even though it had been over two years since her mom passed on, she missed her dearly.

"I sense there's a *but* in there," Nick said softly.

She sighed. "But with Marshal everything is conditional. If I wanted something from him I had to earn it." She blinked back the tears. "In exchange for help with my college expenses, I had to spend my weekends, breaks and summers working for him. He really was hoping I'd take over his business, since neither of his other kids were interested."

"You aren't interested."

"No. And he wasn't happy when I took the job at the station. But I'm not interested in real estate. Especially not now that I could actually get promoted and make some decent money. I'll be able to pay off the last of my loans and then be completely independent from Marshal."

Nick reached over and placed his hand on her knee. "I hope you get that promotion."

"With your help, I will."

The grim set to his mouth and the pensive way his gaze contemplated the fire sent a ribbon of unease unfurling through her. She was acutely aware that he still had the power to pull the plug on this project. Her boss had promised Gordon that he and Nick could review the piece before the story aired, which meant there was still a chance of losing the promised promotion.

Her fate was in Nick's hands.

Determination slid into place. She'd have to make sure he left any and all plugs well enough alone.

The church service ended on a familiar hymn. Nick didn't need to look at the hymnal; the words to "Amazing Grace" were etched in his heart and mind. From his place at the back of the balcony, he couldn't see the congregation below in the nave, but he could hear the voices raised in song. Beside him Julie's soft soprano harmonized with his baritone.

The smile she sent his way as the song ended sent his heart tripping over itself.

"You have a great voice," she commented

and flipped her braid over the shoulder closest to him.

For a moment he was distracted by the fresh sunshine smell of her hair. All through the service he kept catching a whiff of her scent, which provided a pleasant relief to the musty odor of the balcony. "You do, too."

Putting her hand on his arm, she said, "I'm so glad you relented and came with me."

He covered her hand, enjoying the soft, smooth feeling of her skin close to his. "Me, too." He held her gaze. "Talking to you last night helped me, a lot. I really appreciate your willingness to listen and offer wisdom."

"I'm not sure how wise I was, but I'm glad to know my words helped."

"More than helped." After he'd left her in the living room, he'd gone to his room and, for the first time in nearly a year, prayed. He'd poured out his heart to God, giving Him the anguish and pain of losing Cody. And relinquishing the fear of the unknown person wanting him dead. Nick trusted God to protect him and those he cared about. Including the beautiful woman sitting beside him. He liked the way the green of her sweater changed the color of her eyes to a teal that reminded him of the Arabian Sea off the coast of India.

She rose and held out her hand. "You ready to see your parents?"

"I don't think I should go down there. Too many people," he said, though it was nerves, not fear, that had him stuck to the pew.

Julie patted his knee. "I'll bring them to you."

His mouth went dry as she walked away, disappearing down the staircase that would take her to the narthex. She would pass Ted, who'd taken a position at the bottom of the stairs after he'd cleared the balcony.

A few minutes later Nick heard footsteps on the stairs and then his mother's voice.

"What is this about, Julie? You're being so mysterious."

He hissed in a breath as a shaft of pain and longing hit him. It had been too long since he'd seen his mom.

His father noticed him immediately when he reached the top of the stairs. A wide smile broke out on his weathered face and he stepped forward to draw Nick into a fierce hug. "You're all right?" He leaned back to look in Nick's face. "We saw the crash on TV."

"I'm good, Dad," Nick assured him and hugged him again.

His mother's gaze landed on him. The

smile on her face faltered for a fraction of a second, but it was enough to impale Nick's heart.

Disengaging from Dad, Nick said, "Hi, Mom."

"Nick! We'd heard you were in town." She reached for his shoulders and pulled him down to kiss his cheek, just as she had a million times since he was fourteen and had shot past her in height. The familiar gesture formed a lump in Nick's throat.

Dad clapped him on the back. "Why didn't you tell us you'd be home early to compete in the Festival of Snow?"

The subtle reminder of why he'd returned stabbed at Nick. "I meant to. Things have been hectic." An understatement, but now wasn't the time to go into the fact that there was some crazy person out there trying to kill him.

"Are you staying in that ridiculous motor home again?" Mom asked.

Obviously they hadn't heard the news yet. "No. My motor home is out of commission right now. I stayed at Julie's stepfather's home last night."

Dad's black eyebrows rose nearly to his hairline.

Mom's gaze bounced from Nick to Julie. "I see."

Her tone suggested she thought there was more going on than there was, prompting Nick to say, "It's not like that, Mom. I needed a place for the night and Julie offered her stepdad's house."

"You could have come home," Dad said.

The hurt in his father's voice nearly brought Nick to his knees. "It was late. I didn't want to disturb you," he countered, feeling guilty at the lame excuse. He hadn't been sure they'd want him there.

"It's nice of Marshal to let you stay at his house, but you can come home now, right?" Mom asked.

Julie touched Nick's elbow and gave him a gentle squeeze. He didn't need to read her mind to know Julie thought he should stay at Marshal's. The gated community provided a measure of safety that his parents' suburban house wouldn't offer. But how could he say no when his mom was asking him to come home? "Things are complicated right now. I wouldn't want to put you in danger."

"What do you mean?" Dad asked, concern lacing his words.

Nick quickly explained the attempts on his life.

His mother clutched his hand. "Oh, no. Why would someone want to hurt you?"

The genuine distress in her tone washed over Nick, making him feel cared for, loved. Something he hadn't felt from his mother in a year.

"I don't know, Mom. The police are investigating."

"You can at least come home for lunch, right?" Mom asked. "You, too, Julie."

Nick hesitated. The imploring look in his mother's eyes twisted in his chest like a knife. He glanced at Julie. Doubts swirled in her eyes.

"I don't know, Mom. That might not be the best idea."

Dad put his hand on Nick's shoulder. "Son, come home. Let me worry about our safety."

"But, Dad, if either of you was hurt because of me—"

Dad held up a hand. "Stop. We'll be fine. I have my old hunting rifle and we can let the neighbors know to keep an eye out. No one can get in or out of the neighborhood without being seen by someone."

Nick could argue that wasn't true, but then he'd have to admit to sneaking out of the house when he was a teen. Then an image of his father in his striped pajamas patrolling the house with his hunting rifle flashed in his head. All Nick could do was blow out a breath of frustration. "Come on, Dad, you're not really prepared to shoot someone with your shotgun, are you?"

"I'll do whatever's necessary."

Nick rubbed his neck. Regardless of the danger, Nick wanted to go home, to spend some time with his parents. He had a bodyguard. And he refused to live his life like a prisoner, as if he were the one who had done something wrong.

With determination in his voice, he said, "I'd love to come home for lunch."

Worry darkened Julie's expression. "Are you sure you should?"

"I can't live my life hiding like some fugitive." He took her hand. "You don't have to come if you don't want to. Ted and I can go with Mom and Dad."

"You're not getting rid of me that easily. Besides, I think it would be better for your parents to leave here alone and then when the church clears, we can leave."

"That will give us time to go to the grocery store," Mom said.

Dad's confused gaze bounced between them. "Who's Ted?"

"My bodyguard."

"The man guarding the bottom of the

stairs?" Dad asked. "I thought there was something suspicious about him."

Nick chuckled. "He can be intimidating, but he's a good guy."

Mom's eyes widened. "Of course, bring him along."

Dad frowned. "What are the police doing? Why haven't they caught this guy?"

"They're doing their best, Dad," Nick assured him. "You should get going."

"We'll see you two at the house," Dad said and took Mom by the elbow. They descended the stairs.

Julie gave him a satisfied smile. "They were happy to see you."

Tweaking her braid, he said, "Thank you for pushing me to talk to them."

Her direct gaze pierced him with an intensity that made him breathless. "That's what friends are for, right? We help each other out."

*"Friends."* He rolled the word around his mind. Being friends was safe. Uncomplicated. His earlier conclusion that she fell in the frenemy category teetered. "Is that what we are?"

"I think so." Her eyebrows rose. "Don't you?"

In a perfect, less complicated world, he'd

want to be more than friends. But there were so many reasons to keep a distance from this woman that he'd get a cramp in his hand if he tried to write them out. Despite being a reporter, she had made it clear that men like him weren't on her wish list. "Yes, we're friends."

A slight smile touched her lips. "Good."

For some reason he had the distinct impression that she had another reason for making a point of clarifying their relationship.

The church emptied quickly and the parking lot had cleared out by the time Nick, Julie and Ted reached her car at the far end of the lot. Nick reached for the passenger door, but Ted put a halting hand on his arm. "Let me check it for explosives."

Stepping back, Nick swallowed the lump of trepidation clogging his throat.

"Oh, man!" Julie exclaimed from the driver's side.

Heart jumping, his gaze shot over the top of the vehicle at her. "What's wrong?"

Ted rounded the car in a flash. "Flat tire."

Nick came around the front end of the car. Sure enough, the front left tire was deflated. He squatted down to inspect the rubber, thinking she'd run over a nail, but the wide slash on the back of the tire told a different story. "Someone slashed the tire with a knife."

Julie gasped. "I'll call the police." She fumbled to get her phone from her purse.

Ted moved to stand so that Nick was at his back. The bodyguard had withdrawn his weapon and braced his feet apart as if his body could provide a shield to Nick and Julie. Caution tightened Nick's shoulders. He rose and glanced around, looking for a threat. They were the only ones left. He glimpsed the back end of a car parked behind the church. Pastor Harmon must still be inside.

"I don't like how exposed and vulnerable we are standing out in the parking lot," Ted said.

Nick grimaced as the thought slammed into him. They were visible, and other than Ted's gun, they were defenseless. This wasn't such a good idea after all. They should have left when there were other people around. They were going to have to cross fifty feet of open space to reach the church.

Tucking Julie into his side, Nick said, "Let's get inside."

They moved in tandem away from the car, Ted keeping them ahead of him. Something hit the pavement in front of Nick, kicking up bits of blacktop.

Julie yelped. "What was that?"

"We're being shot at!"

# NINE

"Run!" Ted grabbed Nick's shoulder and propelled him forward.

Nick didn't have to hear the command twice. He tightened his hold on Julie and they ran toward the church's front door. More bullets hit the ground. Too close.

When they reached the church door, a bullet slammed into the wood right above Nick's head. But he hadn't heard the loud retort of a gun firing. The sniper was using some sort of suppressor. Ducking, he yanked on the door.

Locked!

"Around back," Ted yelled, searching for the threat.

Grabbing Julie by the hand, Nick pulled her to the other side of the building, out of the line of fire. They hurried to the side door. It was locked, as well.

The sound of an engine turning over drilled panic through Nick.

Julie raced ahead of Nick toward the back of the church in time to see Pastor Harmon driving away.

"Pastor Harmon!" Julie yelled.

The pastor's car continued moving, turning out of the parking lot and driving away.

Nick drew Julie against the wall of the church. "Call the police."

She dialed and frowned. "It's not going through."

"What?" Nick took the phone and punched in 9-1-1. Nothing. "When did you last charge this?"

"Last night." She pointed to the little icon in the top right corner. "See, one hundred percent."

Ted's grim expression sent Nick's pulse into hyperdrive. "The shooter probably has a cell jammer."

"We've got to get inside and use the church's phone." Nick moved to the back door. Ted stood next to Nick with his weapon at the ready.

"It's probably locked, too," Julie said.

Nick inspected the lock. It was similar to the one on the exterior door of his parents' garage. "Do you have two bobby pins?"

"Oh, please." Julie's dubious tone would have made him smile if the situation had been different. "You're going to tell me you know how to pick a lock with a bobby pin?"

Even Ted glanced at him with skepticism.

"Not with one, but two, yes." He kept his gaze alert for any sort of threat. The parking lot remained empty. He could only hope their shooter's position remained facing the entrance.

Julie reached for the back of her head and plucked two bobby pins that had kept a short chunk of hair in place at the beginning of her braid. The shiny strands fell to curve around her cheek. "I'll believe it when I see it."

He bent one of the pins into an L shape, making an Allen wrench, and then inserted it in the base of the lock hole with the longest part in the lock and the small section hanging out. Then he placed one end of the second bobby pin in the top portion of the lock. He jiggled and jiggled while turning the bottom pin with slight pressure until he heard the clicks as the mechanism unlocked.

"Believe it," he said, handing back the pins. He opened the door and ushered her in. They were in Pastor Harmon's office. Julie rushed to the phone on the desk to call the police. Ted shut the door and moved to Nick's side.

"The operator said she'd send help right away." Julie set the receiver down.

The knob of the back door they'd just come through twisted. Gratefully, Nick noted it was a self-locking door.

Julie jumped. Nick clamped a hand over her mouth. "Shh."

Ted pointed toward the exit. "Go. Now."

Taking Julie by the hand, Nick tugged her out of the office. "We're going up to the balcony until the police arrive."

Sunlight came through the stained-glass windows, creating a kaleidoscope of color raining down the center aisle of the sanctuary. Julie, Nick and Ted—bringing up the rear—hurried to the narthex and up the stairs to the balcony.

The sound of wood splintering sent Nick's pulse pounding.

"Find a place to hide," Ted instructed. He crouched down by the railing, then peered over the top. A bullet nearly took him out. Ted fired off a round, the sound bouncing off the walls, before ducking down.

A heightened sense of dread gripped Nick. His throat constricted the way it had the first time he'd tried a double back aerial. He waited with his breath trapped in his chest, knowing any second this whole situation could go south and Julie could end up dead along with him. He moved to the balls of his feet, prepared to launch himself at whoever came at him. He had to protect Julie. She was not going to pay the price for whatever was happening.

The high-pitched wail of a siren filled the church.

A man cursed. Close. On the stairs.

Ted swiveled, his weapon pointed at the mouth of the stairs.

Nick's heart nearly burst from his chest. Then the man retreated, his rapid footfalls booming through Nick like gunfire. It was all Nick could do not to collapse. He grabbed the pew in front of him for support.

The front entrance door crashed open.

"Nick! Nick Walsh!"

Recognizing Detective Agee's gruff voice, Nick scrambled to the railing and peered over. Detective Agee and three officers advanced into the nave, their weapons drawn.

"Here," Nick called out, realizing that if the police were coming through the front the assailant had to have gone out through Pastor Harmon's office. "The shooter went out the back."

Two of the officers hurried forward.

Nick only regretted he hadn't caught a glimpse of the assailant. He went to Julie and helped her up. "You okay?"

She nodded. "Other than my heart being ready to burst out of my chest, yeah, I'm okay."

They met Detective Agee at the bottom of the staircase. Nick let Ted explain the situation to the detective.

"Guy's graduated to firearms," Agee stated grimly. "Did any of you see him?" They all gave a negative response.

The officers returned. "He got away," the youngest of the two officers said. "He's driving a dark blue pickup truck."

"You get the plates?" Agee asked.

"Too obscured with dirt," the other officer reported.

"Get the crime scene techs here," Agee instructed the officers. "Guy had to have left something behind. A shell casing and bullet, at least."

"Yes, sir." Two officers left through the busted front door.

"Where are you staying, Mr. Walsh?" Agee asked.

"He's staying at my stepfather's house with me," Julie answered before Nick had a chance.

"Could you have an officer take us back to the house?" Ted asked. "I'd rather not wait around for the tire to be changed on Ms. Tipton's car."

"Of course." Agee gestured to the remaining uniformed officer. "Officer Comer will drive you. If you think of anything that will help or if anything else happens, call."

Ted ushered Nick and Julie out of the church and to the white City of Bend police cruiser parked at an angle near the entrance. Ted sat up front, while Julie and Nick slid into the back.

Nick had made a promise to his mother he intended to keep. "I need to go by my parents' house first," he told the officer as they headed out of the parking lot.

Ted twisted around to look over his shoulder at Nick. "Mr. Walsh—"

Nick held up a hand cutting of the protest. "We're going to my parents'."

He gave Officer Comer the address.

When they arrived, his parents rushed out of the house. Officer Comer opened the back door for Julie while Ted held the door for Nick. As Nick passed Ted, his bodyguard said, "This isn't a good idea."

The shooter had run when the cops arrived. Nick doubted there'd be another attempt anytime soon, not with the police present. "We won't stay long."

"What's happened?" Mom asked as he stepped up on the porch. "Are you okay? Why are in you in a police car? We were worried."

Hearing the concern and care in her voice was like a balm to his soul. "I'm fine, Mom. We're fine. We had a bit of trouble." He explained about the shooter.

Dad's jaw set in anger. "What are the police doing to find this jerk?"

"Everything they can, Dad."

"You should go inside," Ted instructed with a pointed look at Nick.

Getting the message, Nick took Julie's hand and followed his parents inside. Ted hustled in behind them, leaving the police officer to stand guard on the porch.

The house looked the same, comfortable and lived-in.

"I made your favorite," Mom said. "Orzo Greek salad and crusty bread."

Touched by her effort, Nick didn't have the heart to point out that orzo Greek salad had been Cody's favorite dish. He leaned close to kiss his mother's cheek. "Thanks, Mom."

Mom smiled softly. Her eyes glinted suspiciously with tears. "You're welcome, son. It's good to see you."

He wrapped her in a bear hug. "You, too."

For a long moment he held on. When he let

go and stepped back, his mother turned away and wiped at her eyes. Nick was happy to be home, to be welcomed by his mother and father. But the weight of guilt pressing on his chest wouldn't relent. The unspoken words of forgiveness that he longed to hear never came. The subject of his brother hung in the air like a cold frost, making Nick aware of the missing piece of his family.

After washing up, they sat around the table. Ted's presence provided a silent reminder that this wasn't a normal family gathering. Would life ever be normal again?

Dad said grace, then Julie kept the conversation going, asking his parents questions, talking about mutual friends and local news. Nick was grateful for her presence as a buffer, as a distraction from the grief that floated near the surface.

Needing a moment alone, Nick excused himself and headed down the hall. He paused outside the closed door to his brother's room. Cody's name stenciled on a wooden plaque hung from a hook on the door. Cody had made it at summer camp. He'd been so proud.

Nick's heart ached with loss and sorrow. Compelled by the force of his grief, he opened the door to Cody's room. Needing to remember the boy who'd been the world to their mom, Nick stepped inside. The curtains were drawn, shrouding the room in shadows. Nick flipped on the light, chasing back the gloom. He wished he could do away with the pain squeezing his heart as easily.

Everything about the room made Nick hurt. The room appeared frozen in time, as if waiting for Cody to come home. The double bed with its gray-and-red-striped comforter was made. Cody's high school diploma hung on the wall, along with a collage of photos that Cody had tacked up. There were trophies and books and an old set of skis leaning against the dresser.

A bright green duffel bag sat on the floor. Cody's bag. He'd used it for skiing, keeping his gloves, goggles and hydration pack. He'd had it with him the day he'd died. Someone must have packed it up and shipped it home.

The bottom end of a yellow water bottle stuck out the unzipped top.

Nick squatted down to retrieve the bottle. Water sloshed as he righted it. He stared. It was the same water bottle he'd lost the day Cody had died. How had Cody gotten it?

He wasn't sure what to do with it. Part of him wanted to put it back, leave it with the memories of his brother. Part of him wanted to take it with him as a reminder of the brother he'd lost and as a reminder that he'd caused his brother's death.

Deciding to take it, he left Cody's room and went to his old room.

Unlike Cody's, his room had been redone. A new queen-size bed took up most of the space. New floral bedding had replaced the brown-and-green plaid comforter of his youth. His old desk was gone, and so was his trophy case. The dresser looked different. He inspected it closer and realized it had been refinished. They'd turned his old room into a guest room. He should have guessed when he'd received a box of his yearbooks, photos and other mementos not long after he'd purchased his condo.

When he returned to the living room, his parents and Julie were sitting close together on the couch, looking at a photo album. Ted had taken a position by the door. He had the seen-but-not-heard routine down when he wanted to.

"Please don't tell me that's my baby book," Nick said.

Mom looked up with a smile. "You were the cutest baby."

"I like the pumpkin outfit the best," Julie teased, holding the book up so he could see the photo of him at six months dressed like a pumpkin with a puffy orange body piece and a green sprout on his head.

He shook his head. "I had no say in that."

His mother pointed to the bottle in his hand. "What's that?"

He held it up. "My water bottle."

Mom bolted to her feet. "That's Cody's. You went into Cody's room."

The accusation in her tone hung in the air.

"Evelyn," Dad said as he stood and put a hand on her shoulder. "It's okay."

"No, it's not okay!" she cried and moved quickly away from the couch. "Nothing will ever be okay!"

Nick's heart twisted. "Mom. I didn't mean to upset you."

His mother burst into tears and ran from the room.

Nick felt the world crumble beneath him. He didn't know what to do, how to help her, when he wanted to crawl into the nearest hole and wither away. He looked at his father. "I didn't mean to—"

Dad held up a hand. "You didn't do anything wrong. She's struggling. The closer we get to the anniversary, the more unsettled she is. We'll get through this."

"We should leave," Nick stated, feeling his heart cracking.

"No, please. Give her a moment to gather herself," Dad said. "I'll be right back."

Dad walked out of the living room and down the hall, disappearing into the master bedroom, where Mom had gone.

Nick scrubbed his face with his free hand. His gaze met Julie's. Compassion shone in her eyes. Eyes that glistened with tears. Nick had to look away. "I'm sorry you had to see that."

He heard her set the book on the coffee table and come to him. "Don't be. Family is complicated, and you're all hurting. It's totally understandable. This is a hard time for you and your family. I'm intruding."

He took her hand. "No. You're not intruding." He released her and moved toward the kitchen.

Julie's heart ached with sorrow for what Nick and his parents were enduring. She knew Nick blamed himself. She hated that he did. She wished there were a way to alleviate his pain. But she didn't know how.

He paused at the sink, staring at the yellow plastic water bottle in his hand, looking so forlorn and lost.

She put her arms around his waist and hugged him. Getting too emotionally attached to him wasn't smart, but at the moment she didn't want smart. She wanted to heal, to help, to make him know that he wasn't alone. That she cared.

He set the water bottle in the sink and embraced her, burying his head in the crook of her neck. Silent sobs racked his body.

Seeing him so broken cut her off at the knees. She felt his pain acutely, as if he were transferring the hurt and sorrow directly into her system. She held him and murmured soft words of comfort.

After several long moments, he lifted his head, his blue eyes dark and clouded with sorrow. For a heartbeat she thought he'd push her away again. Instead, he cupped her face with his big, strong hands. His gaze dropped from her eyes to her mouth.

She licked her lips, her heart hammering in her chest. Anticipation tingled through her limbs. He seemed suspended, as if he couldn't bring himself to close the distance.

When his eyes lifted to meet hers again, the withdrawal in the blue depths told her he wouldn't kiss her.

His guilt wouldn't let him take such comfort.

Needing to show him he did deserve comfort, she went on tiptoe and pressed her lips against his. For a moment, his hard mouth felt frozen, cold.

A flutter of panic hit her.

Then he exhaled and melted into the kiss, pulling her flush against him. She lost herself in the sensations bursting through her system like chrysanthemum fireworks. Stars danced behind her eyes, over her limbs. She'd always wondered what it would be like to be kissed by Nick Walsh. Now she knew.

The kiss was better than her teenage heart had ever imagined.

And worse than she'd feared.

# TEN

Slowly, the kiss drew to an end. Julie's senses reeled. Blood rushed to her head, making her dizzy. She nearly lost her balance. Nick placed his hand on her shoulders, grounding her. Through the soft cashmere of her sweater, his hand created hot spots. Judging by the bemused look on his face, he was feeling off-kilter, too.

Nick winced slightly and released her. "I'm—"

She cut him off with a sudden burst of irritation. "If you're going to say you're sorry, I'm going to punch you."

His eyes widened, then a slow grin spread over his face. "Oh, yeah. I'll bet you punch like a girl."

She put her hands on her hips and arched an eyebrow. "I've taken self-defense. I know how to hurt you."

The teasing light in his eyes dimmed. "I'll bet you do."

"Like I could ever do you any harm," she shot back. "I'd probably break my fist."

And he could break her heart, if she wasn't careful.

Uh-oh. Not good. Her heart was becoming attached to him. *Get a grip, girl!* She took a step away, increasing the distance between them.

Gesturing to the bottle in the sink, she refocused on the topic at hand and put her wayward emotions on the shelf, where they needed to stay. "That water bottle was yours?"

He followed her gaze. "Yeah. I had it the day…" A spasm of grief rippled through his expression. "The day Cody died." He visibly gathered his composure. "I'd lost it at some point. He must have found it and stuck it in his bag." He opened the lid. A medicine smell wafted out of the container. "Phew."

Julie took a closer sniff. The fumes stung her eyes. She wrinkled her nose. "That's nasty. Smells like…cherry cough syrup."

"I'd put a vitamin packet in it," he said and tipped the bottle to pour the liquid out. "They must have gone bad."

What if something beside vitamins had been added to the water? A chill of unease raced over her flesh and raised the fine hairs at the back of her neck. "Wait!" Julie put her hand over his. Her stomach knotted. "Do you always put vitamins in your water?"

"Yep. I have a vitamin-B deficiency, so I have to supplement regularly. I get packets from the health food store. It's easier than pills."

Her pulse sped up. "You said you lost the bottle. Where?"

He set the bottle back down, with the liquid still inside. "That was a year ago. It's hard to remember."

Thoughts rattled around her brain, trying to solidify into a coherent idea. "Try."

"I know I filled it in the motor home before heading up the mountain. I thought I put it in my duffel, but I can't be sure. However, when I went to get it, I couldn't find the bottle in the locker or my bag. I figured I must have left it behind. I searched for it later but couldn't find it."

"Could someone have taken the bottle out of your locker or your bag?"

"Maybe. Locker rooms aren't exactly high-security places." He tilted his head. "You think someone took my water bottle? Why would anyone do that?"

"Maybe to put something in it. Something they wanted *you* to drink."

It didn't take long for his quick intelligence to process the implications in her words. He staggered back a step. "You think someone tampered with my water bottle intending to harm me and Cody drank it instead?"

"Think about it. What if Cody's death was actually an attempt on your life?"

The glazed look of denial in his eyes ripped at her heart. "No. Cody died of a broken neck because he tried a trick that he wasn't ready for. My trick."

"But what if he drank from this?" She gestured to the bottle. "Bear with me here. I know it sounds crazy, but then so does someone trying to kill you." She took a breath and slowly calmed her racing heart and put voice to the incredible thought that grabbed a hold of her. "Suppose whatever is in the water disoriented Cody? Impaired him somehow?"

She tugged on the sleeve of his button-down shirt. "Remember, there were witnesses who said he was behaving like he was on something."

"But nothing showed up when they examined his body—" Nick's voice broke on the last word.

Julie hated putting him through this, but

the more she thought about it, the more the idea that Nick had been the one intended to be hurt that day became clear. "There are toxins that won't show up in a routine drug screen, Nick."

He let out a noisy breath. "If what you're saying is true…" He shook his head. "I can't let myself believe—"

"Let's take this to Detective Agee. It's worth checking." And the results could absolve Nick of the guilt he had been carrying around like a weight dragging him down.

For a second he stared into the sink. Then he nodded and reached for the bottle.

"Stop. Put the bottle in a paper bag," Julie said. "Just in case there are fingerprints the police can use."

"You watch too much TV," he commented, but did as she instructed.

"I took a criminal law class when I thought about becoming a lawyer."

"That would have been my next guess."

She smiled, appreciating his quiet sense of humor.

"Let me tell Mom and Dad we're leaving." He handed the bottle to her. "But I'm not going to tell them what we're doing, okay? I don't want to upset them with this needlessly."

"I understand."

He disappeared down the hall while Julie related her theory to Ted in the living room.

"Anything is possible" was his response.

A few moments later Nick returned with his parents following behind. His mom looked tired, her eyes rimmed red and tears staining her cheeks. She walked over to Julie. Julie held the paper bag behind her back with one hand.

"I apologize for my earlier behavior."

"No need to apologize," Julie told her, holding on to the hand Evelyn offered. "I enjoyed lunch. Thank you."

Nick hugged his dad and then his mom. Evelyn held on to him for a moment. "We'll see on you Thursday?"

Nick's Adam's apple bobbed as he swallowed. "Yes, of course."

Evelyn turned to Julie. "We'd love for you to join us. It will be a small, intimate gathering."

Touched by the offer, Julie replied, "Thank you."

Nick ushered Julie out the front door. He was anxious to get the water bottle to the police. They would analyze the contents and determine if there was anything in the liquid besides year-old vitamins. If a substance had been added that had caused Cody to be disoriented and impaired his ability to complete the jump—Nick's heart raced, his thoughts scattered, afraid to allow the possibility of absolution.

Officer Comer was waiting on the front steps. He escorted them to his patrol car and didn't bat an eye when Nick explained they wanted to go to the police station to talk to Detective Agee.

At the station house they found the detective at his desk.

"I was going to call you," he said as he rose from his chair. "We found the van that tried to run you down abandoned on Highway 97. It had been reported stolen two days ago."

The news didn't come as a total surprise. Nick had figured the van would be stolen. He glanced at Ted. By the stoic expression on his face, Nick guessed the bodyguard wasn't surprised, either.

"What about the shooter?" Ted asked.

"We found some casings and pulled bullets out of the balcony railing and the door. No viable fingerprints. The striations on the bullets lead us to believe they were fired from a .223 Remington," Agee said.

"A varmint rifle?" Ted's voice held a note of puzzlement.

"Varmint?" Julie's confused gaze circled the men. "What's that?"

"The .223 Remington isn't a big rifle and is mostly used on small nuisance game like rodents," Agee explained.

Julie wrinkled her nose. "Rats? There's a specific rifle for shooting rats?"

"Rats, squirrels, moles, opossum, raccoon, skunks," Agee explained.

"The rifle is a good choice for small, long-range targets," Ted commented. "The guy must have fashioned some sort of homemade noise suppressor to it."

"Nice. This guy considers me vermin," Nick remarked dryly as images of rats and squirrels marched through his mind, all with his head attached, like little bobble-headed targets.

"Show the detective what we brought," Julie urged Nick.

"We found something which might be relevant." Nick placed the paper bag on the desk and quickly explained Julie's theory that something toxic could have been added to the liquid inside and Cody drank it by mistake.

Eyeing the bag with skepticism on his lined face, Agee said, "That seems a stretch."

"Not really, considering someone's tried

to kill Nick four times now and he received a threatening note," Julie insisted.

Agee's dark eyes considered her. "I'll have the crime lab run the contents to see if they detect anything unusual."

"I'd appreciate you doing that." Thinking Cody's death wasn't just an accident made Nick's stomach ache with more guilt. If it was true that Nick had been targeted and should have been the one to drink the toxic water… then Cody was a victim of a malicious killer. A killer who was still after Nick.

Burning anger chomped through him, making him sweat. "Could you let us know what they find as soon as you can?"

"I will." He tipped his chin to Officer Comer standing a few feet away. "Take them home and keep an eye out."

"Yes, sir," Comer said and motioned for them to precede him out.

"Detective," Ted said, halting everyone. "Did you interrogate the courier guy?"

Eager to hear the answer, Nick retraced the few steps away he'd taken.

"Funny thing about that," Agee said. "First, Thunderbird had no record of sending you anything. And the delivery service said the guy was a new hire and hasn't been seen since he delivered your package, which they don't have a record of, either. The guy gave the delivery service a false name and address."

"Didn't they check him out before hiring him?" Julie asked. "Who hires someone these days without vetting them?"

Agee shrugged. "The ID looked legit and the manager was in a bind and needed someone right away. Though he did say he saw the guy get out of a truck driven by a dark-haired woman. He didn't get the truck's license number."

Julie touched Nick's shoulder. "Kitty?"

He thought about the expression on Kitty's face, a mix of hurt and anger, the first time he'd turned her down. The second time. And the third time…

"Maybe," he answered. "She does seem to be present every time something happens."

"Was she present when your brother died?" Agee asked.

Nick thought back to the week of Cody's death. "I don't recall seeing her. She didn't come around during the week, only on weekends and usually only to competitions, not practices."

"Have you spoken to her?" Ted asked the detective.

Agee inclined his head. "I did."

From the twist of the detective's lips, Nick

figured it hadn't been a pleasant experience. "What did she say?"

"She's a bit off," Agee said. "She definitely has her eye on you and grew really agitated when I suggested she had something to do with the attempts on your life."

Was her agitation from guilt? Nick wondered.

"She's from a very well-respected family in Idaho farming country, according to the local sheriff I talked to," Agee continued. "I can't find anything to link her to your skiing accident."

"But that doesn't mean her fixation hasn't turned deadly," Julie said.

"It happens," Agee said. "Life in the public eye opens the door to obsessive fans. I'll have another chat with her."

Nick flinched as the truth in the detective's words hit him square in the chest. There were numerous athletes, some of whom he was friends with, who'd had their lives threatened by an overzealous fan with delusions of a relationship that didn't exist. Was that the case here?

After a restless night of sleep with dreams of Julie filling his head, Nick left his room and found Ted outside his door. The big guy had propped himself up against the wall, reading a paperback novel. *A Tale of Two Cities* by Dickens, of all things. Nick was developing a soft spot for the guy.

With his shadow in tow, Nick entered the kitchen to find the guys sitting around the table eating breakfast. A stack of pancakes, a plate of bacon and a carafe of orange juice sat in the center of the table. Frank acknowledged him with a tip of the chin. Lee lifted his mug in greeting. Marshal Evans, dressed in a navy suit, crisp white shirt and red tie, sat at the head of the table reading the paper. The man oozed success. No wonder Julie wasn't anxious to try to fill his shoes.

Julie leaned against the counter, drinking from a mug. Her blond hair was pulled back in a low ponytail. She looked fresh and gorgeous in a light peach-colored sweater, tan skirt and knee-high leather boots. Her welcoming smile kick-started his pulse.

"Coffee?" she asked.

He wasn't sure he needed the jolt; his heart was racing purely on seeing her. "That would be nice, thank you."

"Ted?" she asked.

"Thank you," Ted said and took a seat on the bar stool at the counter.

Marshal Evans set the paper aside and

stood to offer Nick his hand. He was a tall man with a head of thick silver hair and a firm handshake. "Hello, Nick. I hope you found your accommodations to your liking."

"Yes, sir. Thank you for allowing us to stay here."

Marshal waved a hand as he lowered himself back to his seat. "Of course. You're welcome to stay as long as you need. We feel pretty safe out here." He made a sweeping gesture to encompass all of the guys. "Help yourselves. The kitchen is fully stocked. I only ask that you pick up after yourselves. Leann, the housekeeper, comes in twice a week, but I don't expect her to do dishes."

"Yes, sir," Frank said with salute.

"That's generous of you," Nick replied with a glance at Julie.

Her lips were pursed as she stared at her stepdad.

"Paper?" Marshal asked, offering Nick a section of the newspaper.

"Please." Nick sat down at the table. The domesticity of sitting down to read the paper with Julie's stepdad made Nick's chest tighten with longing for his own father.

Julie sat down and slid a mug of coffee his way.

"Where's Gordon?" Nick asked.

"He had a meeting with Mr. Davenport," Lee explained.

"Gordon said to tell you he'd be back to pick you up to bring you to the station for the Thunderbird reveal," Julie said.

Frank snorted. "New skins. New skis. So not fair."

Lee elbowed Frank. "Knock it off."

"What?" Frank said. "You can't tell me you don't wish All Good Sports Drink would spring for new equipment."

"Yeah, well, you have a nicer ski jacket than I do, but you don't hear me complaining," Lee groused.

Frank's sponsor was a sports apparel company that specialized in winter gear. Nick shook his head. The two guys were more like siblings than anything else. "I'll ask Mr. Davenport about getting you guys set up with some new skis."

Frank grinned. "Now we're talking."

Lee rolled his eyes at Frank and then turned to Nick. "You don't have to."

"Julie, could you give us a ride up the mountain since we're without wheels?" Frank asked.

"Sure," she said. "I'll be leaving in five minutes."

"What are you driving?" Nick asked.

"My mother's car," she replied.

"You boys can use the Jeep in the garage," Marshal said. "The keys are in the top drawer of the desk in the study."

Nick noted the surprise in Julie's eyes as her gaze shot to her stepdad.

Lee scooted his chair back. "Thank you, Mr. Evans. That's really generous of you." He carried his plate to the sink.

"Yeah, thanks," Frank said and followed Lee's example.

Julie cocked her head. "Thank you, Marshal."

"You're welcome," Marshal said and dropped his gaze back to the paper.

Julie shook her head, her bemused expression making Nick speculate that Marshal's offering to let the guys use one of his cars wasn't something she'd expected. He waited until he walked her to her car to ask about it.

Before he had a chance, Julie beat him to the punch by saying, "I hope that wasn't too uncomfortable." She leaned against the side of her car.

"Uncomfortable? It wasn't at all," Nick said. "Your stepdad was very gracious."

"Marshal practically ignored you."

The annoyed tone in her voice confused Nick. "He offered me half the paper."

"But he hardly said a word other than to tell you not to make a mess."

"He didn't need to. We were bonding over the paper."

"Really?"

"Yes. It's a guy thing."

"If you say so."

"I do. And it was great that he offered to let Frank and Lee use the Jeep."

Her eyebrows dipped together. "Yeah, that was odd. He usually isn't so free with his things."

Nick sensed there was some hurt behind her words. "What's the story between you two?"

Her mouth twisted. "It's a long story and not interesting."

"I'm interested." And he was. He wanted to know everything about her, her hopes, her dreams. Her hurts and heartaches.

"Maybe some other time." She laid a hand on his arm, drawing his attention to where her slender fingers rested. "Has there been any news on the investigation?"

"I haven't heard anything since yesterday, but I plan to stop by the police station to talk to Detective Agee after the Thunderbird reveal."

"Kitty called to set an appointment for her

interview," Julie said. "We'll be meeting this morning. I'll see if I can coax anything useful out of her."

Concern for Julie's well-being arced through him. "Interviewing her isn't such a good idea."

"It will be fine, Nick," she said. "The TV station is very active with lots of people around. I'm not worried about it."

But he was worried. About Julie's safety, about the feelings cascading through his heart and about the way his sense of well-being was tangled up in her.

He was skipping straight past friendship into a realm of emotions that left him gasping for breath as if he'd face-planted in deep powder and couldn't get out.

# ELEVEN

Julie left her stepdad's house while Nick and Ted headed to the community fitness center for a workout. She'd been tempted to stay and join them, but her boss wanted an update, Kitty Rogers was scheduled to come in and Julie needed to get ready for this afternoon's taping with Nick, where Thunderbird would be revealing the skins for his new skis. Plus, Julie still had her regular production assistant duties to attend to.

Driving into town, she tried to wrap her mind around Marshal's behavior. She'd never seen him offer one of his vehicles to anyone, not her or his kids when they came to visit. First he invited strangers to stay and now he was letting them take off in one of his cars. When had he loosened up?

She was still puzzling over that when she arrived at the station a little after eight. The place was humming with activity. One of the many aspects she loved about the job. She made her way through the melee toward her desk. A young man sat there ripping scripts, an old term from days gone by when printers used the long sheets of paper with holes on the side and each sheet had to be torn apart. Now ripping scripts was basically sorting them into various categories.

"Uh, that's my desk," she said, coming to a halt beside the guy who looked to be a few years younger than her. He had brown hair, brown eyes and a tan complexion. His button-down shirt needed an iron's touch.

"You must be Julie." Rising and sticking out his hand, he said, "I'm Bryce Phelps. I'm interning for the next few months. Liam told me to sit here and sort through the scripts for the anchors."

"Okay." She hitched her purse higher on her shoulder. Usually the interns were placed at a table in the back or in an unused conference room. Where was she supposed to work? "I'll be right back."

She found her boss, Liam, in his office.

"Julie, come in." Liam rose as she entered. He was tall and thin with silver-streaked dark hair swept off his forehead. His facial features were narrow with hawklike dark eyes that stared intently as if waiting to spot a weakness. He wore his usual black pants, black turtleneck shirt and black wing tips. He could be intimidating. But she'd learned he hid a soft and sentimental side that came out whenever his grandkids came around. Too bad they were in school right now.

"Uh, why is there an intern at my desk?"

"Because he'll be taking over your PA duties for now and you will be working in the conference room today."

A ripple of excitement gushed through her. Her promotion was within reach. Just a few more takes and then some editing and her feature on Nick would be complete. She bounced on her toes. "That sounds great."

"Everything is set up for the Thunderbird/ Nick Walsh shoot," Liam continued. "Davenport, the Thunderbird CEO, will be here at two to present Nick with a new set of skis."

"Sweet."

At Liam's arched brows, a heated flush rose up her neck. She'd used one of Nick's phrases. He was rubbing off on her in little and big ways. She was not keeping a professional distance. Would Liam notice? To cover her embarrassment, she said, "I'll go set up in the conference room. Is Bob here?"

"He's been in editing since six. He says you've got some good stuff to work with."

Pleased to know that not only did Bob think so, but that he was telling their boss, she said, "Nick has been amazing. I have his self-proclaimed number-one fan coming in at eleven. I'm hoping to get some useful information from her." Julie wanted not only something for her story on Nick but something to help Detective Agee figure out who wanted to harm Nick.

"Good. I'm looking forward to seeing what you've got. When will you have it put together?"

"I hope to have it all formatted and edited together by the end of the week." Best case was to air on Sunday. And maybe do a follow-up once the names of the competitors chosen to travel to the Winter Games were announced.

"All right then. Get it done. I'm counting on this being a home run," Liam said.

"I won't disappoint you," she promised and prayed that was true.

Julie went to the conference room to prep for the day. The lighting in the room was perfect for interviewing. She filled water pitchers and set out a plate of cookies and a bowl

of fruit to provide sustenance in case anyone needed a snack. She arranged two plush
chairs to face each other at the far end of the
room next to the exposed brick wall, creating
a nice intimate setting in which to talk to the
subjects of her interviews.

"Knock, knock."

Julie started as Bob came into the room.
"Hi, Bob. You ready to set up for Kitty Rogers's interview?"

"I sure am." He carried in his camera and
a tripod. "How was your Sunday?"

She blew out a breath. "Wild." She filled
him in on the shooter and the discovery of
Nick's water bottle and her theory that it
could possibly be tainted.

"Wow. I'm glad you weren't hurt," he said,
concern darkening his gaze.

"Me, too." Julie's gaze shot out the door to
land on the petite woman talking to Bryce.
She wore a red top that dipped in a low V, a
tight black skirt that stopped above the knees
and high heels. She looked ready for a night
out rather than an interview. "Kitty's here."

"I'll be ready in two minutes," Bob said,
setting up the tripod.

After stowing her purse, Julie walked over
to where Kitty was talking with Bryce. The
young intern hung on Kitty's every word,

apparently smitten by a case of puppy love. "Hello, Kitty."

Kitty's smile cooled. She hitched the leather strap of her purse higher on her shoulder. "Hello, Miss Frost. I'm ready for my interview."

"Of course you are." Julie gestured toward the conference room. "Right this way."

Julie led Kitty to the two plush chairs. Taking the seat facing the wall, Julie waited for Kitty to settle into the opposite seat. Bob clipped a microphone to Kitty's shirt.

A flutter of anxious nerves hit Julie's tummy. She needed this to go well. She glanced at Bob. He gave her a nod, letting her know he was ready. Turning to Kitty, Julie smiled and said, "Comfortable?"

Kitty's wide-eyed gaze stared over Julie's shoulder at the camera. "I guess. Yes. Do I look okay?"

Figuring that question was aimed at Bob more than her, Julie waited.

Bob gave Kitty the thumbs-up sign. "You look good."

Kitty sat back and visibly relaxed a bit. "Okay." Her gaze went to Julie. "Now what?"

"Why don't you tell us about yourself?" Julie suggested.

For the next fifteen minutes Kitty talked,

running Julie through her life, explaining various familial relationships that made Julie dizzy. Apparently the Rogerses were deeply entrenched for many generations in the Wood River Valley town of Hailey, Idaho.

Julie knew they wouldn't use a fraction of what had been recorded. Bob had even poked Julie in the back, which Julie interpreted to mean he wanted Julie to hurry Kitty along. But Julie chose to let Kitty have her moment. Maybe in her ramblings she'd reveal something useful.

Finally Kitty took a breath, allowing Julie to interject, "So how did you become interested in Nick Walsh and following his career?"

"Two years ago the U.S. freestyle competition was held at Sun Valley. That's just up the way from where I live. So a bunch of us went to watch. It was the first time I'd seen the aerial competition live. It was breathtaking. And Nick was..." Kitty sighed. "Dreamy. And I was hooked. I've attended every competition I could since then."

"That's dedication. What does your family think of your—" Julie stopped herself from saying *obsession*. "Of your fascination with Nick?"

Kitty grimaced. "Mom understands, but Dad and the rest think it's silly. My sister,

Jeannie, is always teasing me. But I don't care. This is what I want to do."

"How do you finance your trips?"

"I started a catering company right out of high school. I do well especially during the summer and wedding season."

There were depths to Kitty Julie hadn't guessed. "You're an entrepreneur. I like that. What's the name of your company?"

"Gourmet Kitty. My logo is a white cat wearing a ruffled apron. My friend Troy's an artist and he created it for me." Kitty opened her purse and took out a postcard-size advertisement for her company. "Here."

Julie was impressed with both the design and Kitty. "Have you always loved to cook?"

"Cooking is my passion. I'm at home in the kitchen."

"It must be hard running a business and traveling all over the place to watch the freestyle competitions."

"Not really. I set my own schedule, so when there's a competition within a day's drive, I don't take on a job during that time."

"You drive to all the competitions?"

"Yes. I'm not big on flying."

"You must get lonely traveling alone like that."

"Oh, I'm not alone. Someone always comes

with me. My brother, Andy, or my sis, Jeannie, will ride along. Or a friend. Sometimes a bunch of us will pile in the car and take the road trip to Utah, Colorado or even to Canada."

Admittedly surprised by the number of—okay, she'd say it—seemingly normal relationships in Kitty's life, Julie had no choice but to reevaluate Katherine "Kitty" Rogers. "So as Nick Walsh's number-one fan, what can you tell me about him?"

Kitty's eyes lit up. "He's one of the nicest guys on the circuit. Some of the guys are players who like to party when they are off the slopes. But not Nick. He's a straight shooter, as my dad would say. I rarely see him in the bars or trendy nightspots. He's also a gentleman. Really respectful and all." The longing on her face made Julie's stomach cramp. "He's the kind of guy every girl dreams of marrying."

Thoughts of Kitty marrying Nick twisted Julie up inside. Scrubbing the image from her mind, Julie kept her smile firmly in place.

Kitty's gaze narrowed on Julie. "He's also the kind of guy who won't settle down. He needs a woman willing to live in the moment. Someone who will wait for him while he's traveling the world competing. Someone he can come home to and know he'll always be her priority."

Julie had no doubt Kitty thought that person should be her. Deciding not take the bait, Julie switched the subject to the one that mattered the most to her.

"Do you have any idea why someone would want to hurt Nick?"

Kitty blinked. "The police asked me that, too. Nick's the best at what he does. Even his brother, who was good, couldn't beat Nick. There are lots of guys out there who want to be Nick."

"Can you think of someone who wants to bring Nick down?"

Shaking her head, Kitty said, "No one specifically. I mean, I have never heard anyone talk bad about him. Everyone likes Nick, as far as I can tell."

"Were you there when Nick's brother, Cody, had his accident?"

Kitty shook her head. "That was so sad. Nick dropped out of sight for a few weeks afterward. I was so worried about him. I tried to find him... But he bounced back and now he's all set to win gold next month."

"You sound confident," Julie remarked.

"Who do you think will be his biggest competition?"

The gleam in Kitty's eyes made it clear she was pleased to be asked. "There are several excellent aerialists on the U.S. team, but I don't really think any of them could outdo Nick. His main rivals will come from China, Canada and Belarus."

As Kitty went on in great detail about the aerialists from each country, Julie found herself more and more impressed. Not only did Kitty know their stats, current scores and standings, but she also related personal information about each skier that would have required more than simple internet research.

There was more to Kitty than Julie had thought. She wondered why Nick had never given Kitty a chance.

And just as quickly as the thought formed, Julie had to admit she was glad he hadn't. She chose not to examine why.

When Kitty ran out of steam, Julie jumped in, ready to wrap up the interview. "You are a fascinating woman, Kitty Rogers. I'm so glad we had a chance to talk to you. I'm sure our viewers will find your observations interesting."

Obvious pleasure lit up Kitty's dark eyes. "Thank you for having me. Will Nick be here soon? I know he's supposed to be interviewing with you today."

Julie leaned forward. "How did you know that?"

Kitty's brow furrowed. "I heard it somewhere." She shrugged as she unclipped the microphone. "You know how it is. People talk. Especially within the skiing community. All the skiers know me." As if stating an indisputable fact, Kitty stood, placed the microphone on the chair and headed for the door.

Julie hurried to catch up with her and escorted her out of the conference room. "Bryce," Julie called. "Would you walk Kitty out?"

The eager expression on the young intern's face was priceless. "Sure thing."

Julie turned to Kitty and shook her hand. "Thank you for coming today. If you could leave your contact info with Bryce, I'll be in touch to let you know when the piece will air."

Kitty's gaze slid to Bryce. "I can do that."

Bryce led Kitty back to the desk. Kitty sat on the edge and leaned toward Bryce while he wrote down her information. The woman was a flirt. Julie felt sorry for any man who tried to tame Kitty.

Suddenly the air behind Julie grew charged and a deep voice rumbled in her ear, "Hey, beautiful."

Nick surprised her even more when he slid an arm around her waist, pulling her up close.

Julie let out a startled squawk and twisted in his arms. She placed her hands on his chest. The navy cotton sweater stretched taut over his muscles. "Hi. You're early. How was your workout?"

Over Nick's shoulder, she saw Ted standing a few feet away, dressed in a black suit and looking intimidating.

"Good. I hope it's okay we're here now," Nick said. "I was bored and since Ted wouldn't let me go up the mountain and get a run in, I thought I'd come see if you're free for lunch."

Her breath caught. Torn between her desire to say yes and her need to keep things strictly professional, she hesitated and gazed into his eyes, searching for something to give her the strength to resist him. She found herself only more enthralled. "Yes," she said softly. "I'd love to have lunch with you."

His gaze dropped to her lips. For a heartbeat she feared and hoped he'd kiss her. Her lips tingled. Her fingers flexed, pressing into his muscled chest.

"Nick!"

Kitty's sharp tone broke through the haze of yearning tugging Julie toward a course of action there would be no returning from. Abruptly, she stepped back, forcing Nick to relinquish his hold on her.

Annoyance crossed Nick's face before his expression settled into politeness. "Hello, Kitty. Did your interview go well?"

Kitty's dark gaze bounced between Nick and Julie and back to Nick. "Yes. It was enlightening."

Julie wasn't sure how Kitty had been enlightened. "Kitty is quite knowledgeable about many things. Did you know, Nick, Kitty is an entrepreneur?"

"No, I didn't." His polite, uninterested gaze met hers.

"She owns and operates a catering company. Her passion is cooking," Julie offered, watching to see how he'd react.

His expression didn't change as his gaze slid to Kitty. "Nice."

"I was just leaving, Nick. Would you be a love and walk me out?" Kitty asked, her lips pulled back in something that wasn't quite a smile.

Nick's eyebrows twitched. "Actually, Jules and I can walk you out. We're on our way to lunch."

Kitty shot Julie a withering glare. "Thank you."

Julie met Bryce's confused gaze and waved him off. He shrugged and walked away.

"Just let me grab my purse," Julie said and hurried back toward the conference room to retrieve her bag from the cabinet where she'd stored it. Taking a moment to steady herself, she prayed for guidance and strength to resist her attraction to Nick. A noise behind her sent her senses on alert. She spun around. Kitty and Nick stood inside the doorway.

Nick stepped past Kitty to reach for Julie's hand. "Ready?"

Hurt crossed Kitty's face. She bit her bottom lip and her eyes glistened suspiciously.

Julie felt sorry for her. Then Kitty's expression cleared, her gaze hardening. She turned on her heels and marched toward the stairs.

At Nick's questioning look, Julie lifted a shoulder. "Guess she decided she didn't need us to walk her out."

They'd agreed on an Italian place a few doors down from the station. The walk over cooled Nick's temperature as well as his thoughts. He hadn't expected to react to seeing Julie the way he had. He hadn't realized how much he'd missed her in the short time they were apart. His heart had lurched and his blood hummed.

He'd almost kissed her in her place of work, which would have been unprofessional as well as dangerous. He was letting himself get too attached to Julie.

Letting their relationship progress any further would only end in a disaster. He wasn't looking for a long-term commitment, and Julie was the type of woman who would expect—who deserved—more than he was willing to give. She'd made it clear he wasn't the type of man she needed in her life. He would respect that.

When he left in a few days, he wanted to part on good terms, not with either of them smarting from an ill-advised romance.

Nick held out Julie's chair for her to sit at the table in the back corner of the restaurant, away from the windows and prying eyes. Ted sat at a table to their right, where he had a good view of the restaurant and could see any threats coming.

Taking the seat opposite Julie, Nick noticed the way she tugged on her bottom lip and the uncertainty in her eyes. "Is something wrong?"

She moistened her lips. His gaze tracked the movement and his gut tightened. The waitress set menus and glasses of water down on the table.

As soon as the waitress walked away, Julie picked up her menu. "What would you like?"

*To kiss you. Again.* "Lasagna."

"Good choice."

He held her gaze across the top of the menu. Her bright eyes drew him in, stirring his blood. Something shifted in the vicinity of his heart. His breath quickened. Yes, she was a good choice. A quality woman. Kind and gentle, smart and generous. A woman worth loving.

He swallowed back that thought. Love wasn't on the menu. Or was it?

Lunch with Nick had been enjoyable. He'd charmed Julie with his stories about the ski world. It was such a foreign life to her. Always traveling, going from one ski resort to the next. The competitions and the rivalries. The drama and the adventure. She didn't know how the families of elite athletes coped with the long stretch of the competitive season year after year.

It was a good thing she had no intention of letting herself fall for Nick. She'd never be content in that sort of lifestyle.

They arrived back at the television station before Mr. Davenport. Bob was waiting in the conference room.

"Let's get Nick set up with the microphone," Julie said to Bob.

"Hey, Julie!" Bryce hurried to her side, carrying a large manila envelope. "This was delivered for you."

She took the envelope. Her name was written on the outside, but there was no address or stamp. "Who delivered it?"

Bryce shrugged. "I dunno. Reception sent it up."

"Thanks." She moved to the conference table to open the envelope and pulled out the contents. A photograph. Of Nick. Receiving an injection by a nurse.

Frowning she turned the photo over. Nothing was written on the back. No help there. She once again looked at the image in her hand.

Someone had been trying to harm Nick.

Her stomach dropped.

Or was this picture proof that Nick was already harming himself?

* * *

Nick noted the color drain from Julie's face as she looked at whatever she'd been handed.

"Have a seat," she said, gesturing to the chair facing the camera. She sat down and without preamble handed him the manila envelope in her hand. "This was just delivered to me."

The grim expression in her eyes sent a shiver of foreboding down the nape of his neck. He opened the envelope, slid out the contents and stared at the image before him. He recognized Annie, the nurse at his doctor's office in Lake Placid. "I don't understand. What is this?"

Lifting his gaze, he saw the speculation in Julie's eyes. His gaze drifted to the black lens of Bob's camera. The air in his lungs expanded until he thought his ribs would pop apart. He'd been ambushed. On camera.

"Julie, this is not what it looks like."

"I hope not, Nick. I really hope not."

# TWELVE

"Are you doping?" Julie asked, her gaze direct, her tone impersonal, as if she was asking about the weather instead of a morally charged question.

He recoiled from her inquiry as hurt and offense crowded in, making his fingers curl into fists, crumpling the photo. "You don't pull punches."

"A picture of you receiving an injection looks bad. With the use of steroids by top athletes now so prevalent in the media..." Her voice trailed off, but the implication was clear. She thought he was using performance enhancers to up his edge in competition. The rules were strict and the pressure was on for all the athletes hoping to make the U.S. team and vying for the gold.

"I have never failed a drug test," he stated through clenched teeth. Dropping the mashed photo onto the floor, he unhooked the microphone from his collar as he rose from his chair then stalked toward the door.

Julie hurried around the other side of the conference table to cut him off before he could exit. "Nick, please don't go."

He stared at her through a cloud of anger. "Do you really believe I would dope?"

"No," she answered quickly. "No, I don't."

He wasn't convinced. "Then why ambush me?"

"Because I wanted the world to see your genuine reaction."

Resentment reared up. "Did you get what you were after?"

"Yes, Nick. You gave me the answer I was hoping for."

She had wondered, then, if he was capable of cheating. Did she still? Hurt clawed at his throat.

She smoothed the photo and placed it on the table next to him. "Tell me what this is. Please."

"I told you I have to keep my vitamin stores up." He tapped the image of himself. "This is me getting a vitamin B12 shot almost a year ago. I have a condition called pernicious anemia, which basically means I have trouble absorbing vitamin B12 from food. The committee knows. I've been up front with them about the condition from the beginning."

"Okay."

Pressure expanded in his chest. "Okay?"

"I believe you, Nick."

Her words soothed him way more than he'd have thought.

"How long have you had this condition?" she asked.

He blew out a tense breath. "A couple of years."

"Why is this the first we've heard of it?"

Curling one corner of his lip, he said, "We? You mean the public?"

She grimaced. "Yes, the public."

"HIPAA." He sighed. "And because I don't go around talking about it." And he didn't want to now. Dread bunched his nerves together. "What are you going to do with the photo, Jules?"

Seconds of tense silence passed before she said, "Shred it."

Relief swept over him like an avalanche. "You said someone delivered this?"

Her eyes were troubled when she answered. "That's what the intern said."

Nick rubbed the back of his neck, but he couldn't wipe away the anxiety chasing down his spine. Someone had been spying on him.

He didn't need to see the photo again to recall the image. From the angle and the background, he'd guess the picture had been taken from the window. He'd been followed to his doctor's office. Whoever had taken the picture had hung on to it for almost a year and then sent the photo to Julie, clearly expecting her to use it in her feature on Nick as a way to discredit him. Obviously since the attempts on his life had failed, whoever wanted to hurt him had resorted to ruining his reputation.

He wasn't sure which scared him more.

Julie hated that she'd hurt Nick. When she'd opened the envelope and pulled out the picture, she'd wanted to rip it up, but then she'd realized getting his initial reaction on tape would be huge for her feature story as well as a way for the public to see Nick unguarded and unprepared. He'd given her the answer, the reaction she'd hoped and prayed for. "We need to know who sent the picture."

Nick stared at her a moment, as if deciding whether to trust her. She waited, knowing there was nothing she could say now. He'd have to make the decision on his own. Finally, he said, "Yes, we do."

"Let's go talk to the receptionist," she said, grabbing the photo and the envelope.

They left the conference room. Ted stood outside the door and fell into step behind them as they hurried to the first floor, making a beeline for the reception desk.

"Sherry, who delivered this?" Julie held up the manila envelope.

In her late fifties, Sherry Smith blinked up at Julie through thick glasses. Her red lips puckered in annoyance. "I didn't get a name."

"What did the person look like?"

Sherry's brow wrinkled. "What am I, 4-1-1? I didn't really look at him. The phones were going crazy when he dropped that off."

"At what time?"

On a huff, Sherry replied, "Just after noon."

Frustration tightened a knot in Julie's chest. She glanced up at the security camera near the door. "Come on."

She led Nick and Ted to the security room at the back of the building. One security guard sat in a chair in front of a TV monitor. He was eating a hamburger from a fast-food restaurant.

"Kevin," Julie said.

He swiveled in his chair to face her, his hazel eyes widening, his gaze bouncing between the three of them. He swallowed. "You startled me."

"Sorry." She stepped closer. "Hey, a guy

hand delivered a piece of mail for me around noon. Can you show me the recording of the front desk at that time?"

Wiping his mouth with a napkin, Kevin set his food down on a brown paper bag. "Sure." He fiddled with the monitor. The images on the screen changed. The front desk came into view. Sherry was fielding calls. A moment later the front door opened. A man walked in. He had a peculiar, uneven gait and his shoulders hunched. A ball cap was pulled low over his face and he kept his chin tucked in. He wore jeans and a plaid shirt. No coat, which seemed strange considering the cold temperature. The guy must have been freezing, yet he'd come in without any outerwear.

He set the manila envelope on the desk and ambled out, not even waiting to speak to Sherry.

"Does he look familiar?" Ted asked Nick.

Nick shook his head. "No, he doesn't."

"Can you make me a copy of this, please?" Julie asked Kevin.

Two minutes later, they left the security room with a slim thumb drive.

"We need to take this to Detective Agee," Julie said, holding up the thumb drive. "We could be looking at the man who's trying to kill you."

* * *

The next morning Julie was putting the finishing touches on her makeup when a pounding at her bedroom door drew her attention. The incessant knocking sounded urgent, and anxiety cramped her stomach. She hurried to open the door.

Nick stood there with a copy of the local newspaper in his hand. "Did you see this?"

She stared at the picture on the front page of the *Bend Daily News*. It was the same photo that had been delivered to her at the television station. The caption read, Local Hero Suspected of Doping.

Gripping the edge of the door, she lifted her gaze to meet Nick's. The anger and hurt in his eyes speared through her. "I didn't have anything to do with this."

His eyebrows pinched together. "I didn't say you did. But obviously you weren't the only one who received a copy of the picture."

She took the paper from him and quickly read the article. "This is all supposition and insinuation. There's nothing of substance here." She noted the name of the reporter on the byline. Anger churned in her gut. "He didn't do his due diligence."

"In my experience, reporters don't care for the truth. They only want to sensationalize anything that can look like a scandal, no matter how off base they are," Nick said with a lethal dose of bitter resentment in his tone.

She straightened. "That's not fair. Not all reporters are unscrupulous. I would never do that."

"Then you probably won't make it in your chosen profession," he said. "This is what sells."

As much as she wanted to argue with him, he was right. The public at large gobbled up scandal like candy. "You need to refute it. We can go to the studio today and you can set the record straight."

He ran a hand through his hair. "The damage is done. I can't even imagine what my family thinks."

She shook the paper. "You can counteract this. Set the record straight. If you hide your health issue, then the world is going to think you're ashamed." She wished she could make him understand. "Nick, there's no shame in needing medical help."

"Maybe."

The doubt in his tone knotted her chest. "Nick, trust me. We'll make this right." She stared at the photo again. "Detective Agee's working on finding the guy that dropped the picture off at the television station. He can check with the paper to see if the same guy delivered the photo there."

"I'll call him." He stepped back. "I need to get out of here. I need to see my parents and make sure they know this is a lie."

"Let me grab my purse and I'll come with you."

"I'd rather you didn't," he said. "I need some space."

Hurt ripped through her. "You'll come to the station after you see your parents?"

Tipping his head back slightly, his gaze on the ceiling, he blew out a breath. When he met her gaze, the lack of emotion in the blue depths sent a fissure of worry chomping through her. "I don't know. The damage has been done. Just like Cody, there will always be this cloud hanging over me now."

"Nick—"

The trill of her cell phone filled the air between them.

"I'll talk to you later."

It took effort not to follow him. Her heart ached with anger on his behalf. With a sigh, she retrieved her phone from the bedside table.

"What happened?" Liam's irritated voice assaulted her when she answered the phone. "How did the *Bend Daily* get the scoop when you've spent the last four days with Nick Walsh?"

"It's not a scoop, it's a fabrication made up of speculation and innuendo."

"That picture is condemning," he said. "How do you know it's not true?"

"Because I asked," she shot back. "The photo isn't the whole story."

"And you're going to get the whole story, right?" Liam asked.

"I— Yes." One way or another she would work the truth into the feature on Nick. She had his genuine reaction denying that he was doping on camera. That was a start. A good start.

"Good. Okay." Liam sounded mollified. "That's good. Glad you're on top of it." He hung up without saying goodbye.

Mulling over the situation, Julie went into the kitchen and stopped short when she saw her stepdad sitting at the dining table drinking coffee. He had on his usual business attire. Navy suit, crisp white shirt, red tie. "Hi, I didn't realize you were here," she said.

"It is my house," he commented without looking up from the paper he had spread across the table.

Stung by his abrupt manner, she sipped from her mug, her gaze going to the window and the view of the pond beyond the snow-covered lawn. Her feature story on Nick wouldn't air for a few more days. Until then the world would believe the report in the paper, just as the world had believed his brother had been high on something when he had his accident. The more she thought about the water bottle found in Cody's things, the more she believed the liquid had been tainted. She hated how long it was taking the forensic people to analyze the contents. Reality wasn't anything like they made it out to be on TV.

"You're pale. Are you all right?"

Her gaze shifted to Marshal. Surprised that he'd noticed, she shrugged. "Not really."

"Does it have something to do with your friend and the picture in the paper?"

"Yes, actually." She set her mug down. "It's not fair. He's done nothing wrong, but public opinion will convict him of wrongdoing without a trial."

"What are you going to do about it?" Marshal asked.

"Me?" What could she do?

"Yes, you. You care about him, don't you?"

"Of course, he's my friend."

Marshal dipped his chin and stared at her. "Friend? I've seen the way you look at him. You're smitten."

"Smitten?" she repeated, stifling a smile at his choice of words. Words that reverberated through her like a bouncy ball, punching holes in all the carefully erected walls around her heart.

"Yes, smitten." Marshal folded the paper and laid it on the table. He steepled his hands. "Julie, if you believe your friend is being maligned unfairly, then you need to lead the charge in making sure the world knows the article is full of falsehoods."

His words tumbled around in her head. Since the feature on Nick wouldn't be airing right away, there was only one thing for her to do—write a letter to the editor refuting the newspaper's bogus story.

"Thank you, Marshal. I know what I need to do," she said, rising from the table.

He inclined his head. "You always do, Julie. You always do."

Her breath stalled. "Do you mean that?"

His eyebrows rose. "Of course. You're a smart woman with a good head on your shoulders. Your mother would be so proud of you. I'm proud of you."

Overwhelmed by the magnitude of his statement, she impulsively hugged him.

When he hugged her back, tears sprang to her eyes.

After a long moment, she pulled away and wiped at the moisture on her cheeks.

"Hey now, I didn't mean to upset you," Marshal said, concern etched on his face.

"You didn't upset me. You made me very happy," she said as love and gratitude smoothed the edges of her hurt and softened her heart toward him. She prayed this was the beginning to a new and better relationship with her stepdad. "These are tears of joy."

He stared at her dubiously for a moment, then gave her a soft smile and nodded. "All right, then. Go fight for your man."

She saluted and retreated to her room. It didn't take her long to write a scathing letter, calling out the reporter and the newspaper for not doing their due diligence and fact-finding.

She put the letter in an envelope and stuck it in her purse. She would drop it off on her way in to work.

The drive to town took longer than she'd expected. Lots of traffic coming off the mountain. Before handing over the envelope to the receptionist at the *Bend Daily News* office, she hesitated as second thoughts bombarded her. How would her boss react when he found out she'd sent the note? Was defending Nick's reputation worth risking her promotion? Why did she feel this overwhelming sense of need to right this wrong when he wasn't willing to do it himself?

The answer that gushed up from deep in the depths of her heart made her stagger back a step.

She'd fallen in love with Nick.

Against all reason and logic, she'd allowed him into her heart. She wasn't just smitten. She was doomed.

When Julie entered her office, she found Kitty Rogers waiting at the reception desk.

"What can I do for you, Kitty?" Julie asked as the woman followed Julie up the staircase.

"I need to know where Nick is," Kitty said. "I want to make sure he's okay. He wouldn't do something like what the newspaper is accusing him of."

Julie stopped halfway up the staircase and turned to Kitty. "I don't know where Nick is right now. I'm not his keeper."

"Of course you're not," Kitty huffed. "I don't know who else to ask, though. He's not answering his phone and I can't find him at any of the hotels in town."

"How did you get his cell phone number?"

"A friend."

Julie crossed her arms over her chest.

"Look, you need to know that Nick's not interested in you."

The hard glint Julie had previously only seen glimpses of settled firmly and frighteningly on Kitty's face.

"Don't think you're going to get your claws into him," Kitty said through clenched teeth. "I won't let you. He's mine. He just hasn't realized he needs me yet."

A sudden coldness hit Julie at the core. "What do you mean he hasn't realized he needs you?"

Kitty's lip curled. "He will, given enough time. But you need to back off."

The coldness turned to stone-cold anger. Julie advanced on the other woman. "Are you the one trying to hurt Nick?"

Kitty's eyes widened and she stepped back. "What? No, of course not."

Julie glanced up to see Bryce hovering at the top of the stairs.

"I think you should leave now, Kitty," Julie said.

Kitty swung around in a huff, hitting Julie hard with her purse in the process. Julie lost her balance and teetered on the edge of the stair. Her fingers flexed around the railing just as her foot slipped off the stair. She stumbled down several steps while still clinging to the railing, wrenching her wrist, and the resulting pain made her cry out. Regaining her balance, she leaned against the wall.

Bryce hurried down the stairs. "Are you hurt?"

Kitty rushed to her side, the picture of contrition. "I'm so sorry. I didn't mean to make you fall. Are you okay?"

Cradling her throbbing wrist, Julie said, "I twisted my wrist. I need some ice."

"I'll get you some," Bryce said and ran back up the stairs.

"Uh, I should go," Kitty said and hurried down the steps, the rapid fire of her heels echoing off the walls.

Slowly, Julie made her way to the conference room.

Bryce brought her a bag of instant ice from the first aid kit. "Here. Put this on your wrist."

Molding the bag around her wrist, Julie winced. After a few seconds, the cold seeped through her skin to numb the pain.

"You should have that looked at," Bryce commented.

Bob stepped into the room. "Hey, what happened?"

"Kitty Rogers pushed her down the stairs," Bryce said.

Julie shook her head. "She didn't push me.

She accidently hit me with her purse and I lost my balance."

"It sure looked deliberate to me," Bryce commented.

"Let me see," Bob insisted, reaching for her wrist.

She removed the ice pack and scrunched up the sleeve of her sweater. Her right wrist was turning a nasty dark purple and was already swollen.

"Come on, let's take you to urgent care," Bob said, placing a hand under her elbow. "You could have a hairline fracture or something."

Great. Just what she needed.

Was Bryce right? Had Kitty deliberately hit Julie with her purse, intending to knock her off balance?

Had Julie become Kitty's target?

"We're glad you came over and cleared this up," Nick's father said. "We weren't sure what to think when we saw the photo in the paper."

Nick's lung constricted, making it hard to take a full breath. He sat on the couch next to his dad. Mom sat on the leather ottoman, so close her knees touched his. His gaze bounced between them. "You have to believe me. I would never cheat."

"Of course you wouldn't," Mom said, clearly offended on his behalf. "This article is bogus. My boys wouldn't do drugs."

"No, we wouldn't, Mom." Nick's heart twisted in his chest. Only Cody wasn't here to defend himself. Julie's words replayed in his head. *You can counteract this. Set the record straight.*

She was right. He needed to publicly set the record straight. If people chose to believe the worst, then so be it. As long as the people he cared about believed in him, that was all that mattered.

"So this condition you have," Dad said. "Is there a cure?"

"I have to manage my vitamin intake. It's not that uncommon. And not life threatening as long as I am aware of the symptoms and stay on top of my B12 intake. It's really not a big deal. Please don't worry."

"That's good to know," Dad said. "But worry we will. We love you, son."

Mom clutched his hand. Tears welled in her eyes. "I couldn't stand it if something happened to you."

He gave her hand a squeeze. "Nothing's going to happen to me."

His cell phone rang. Using his free hand, he dug it out of his jacket pocket. The caller

ID said Bend Police. His chest knotted. Had something happened to Julie? No, it had to be Agee calling with the results of the forensic test on his water bottle. He answered.

"Nick, Agee here. I have some news. The liquid in the water bottle you brought in had a high amount of diphenhydramine."

Nick's mouth went dry. Julie had been right. Cody's death *wasn't* an accident.

# THIRTEEN

"**W**hat is *di-phen-hi-dra-mean?*" Nick asked, his mind staggering to comprehend what the detective was telling him. He met his mom's curious gaze and his heart tumbled. How was he going to tell her Cody's death wasn't an accident but a botched attempt at hurting her eldest son?

"Benadryl. Basically, someone poured a bottle of liquid Benadryl into your water bottle. It would have made you dizzy, fatigued, and if enough had been ingested, caused hallucinations. We'll reopen the investigation into Cody's death."

Feeling as if he was going to be sick, Nick thanked the detective and hung up. Telling his parents was difficult, but he forced the words out. His mother's tears impaled him.

"It should have been me," he said, hanging his head.

"No!" Dad slid his arm around his shoulders. "It shouldn't have been anyone."

His mother moved to sit on his other side and wrapped her arms around him. She didn't speak, just hung on to him.

They remained that way for a long time, each mourning the loss of Cody. Healing also.

Gathering his composure, Nick said, "I need to tell Julie she was right. It was her idea to test the water bottle." He owed her so much. If she hadn't stopped him from dumping the liquid out and insisting they take it to the police, the evidence would have been lost forever. Now they knew Cody wasn't high or drunk. He'd been poisoned with too much antihistamine.

"She's a smart lady," Dad said.

"Yes," Nick said. Smart and funny and caring. "Yes, she is."

"I like her," Mom said. "In case you were wondering."

"Mom." Nick could see the matchmaking wheels turning in his mother's eyes. Better than the grief and pain. "We're just friends."

Mom gave an indelicate snort. "The way you two were looking at each other, I'd say it's long past friendship."

Growing uncomfortable with the direction the conversation was heading, Nick said, "I'm

not ready for commitment. Julie's a commitment type of woman."

"You're not getting any younger," Mom replied. "You let her slip away, you might never
find someone who's as perfect for you."

Nick looked to his dad for help.

Dad smiled. "I like Julie, too."

Great, they were ganging up on him. He
wished Cody were here to take some of the
pressure off him. A sharp stab of grief hit
him. "I have to finish what I've started. I can't
let a relationship derail my quest for gold. I
owe it to Cody."

Mom took his hand. "But there's so much
more to life than a chunk of metal."

"Your mom's right, Nick," Dad said, his
voice low, intense.

"I'm not going to give up on my dreams
like—" Nick stopped himself in time from
saying *you*.

When Nick was nineteen, he'd found a trophy and a silver medal in a glass case tucked
away in the attic. Dad had admitted they were
his. He'd been a champion Super-G skier back
in the day. He'd given up his dreams of gold
to marry Mom. Nick had decided then and
there he'd never let romance get in the way
of his dreams.

"Hold up a second," Mom said, her gaze

narrowed on Nick. "Is that crack aimed at your father?"

Nick's face flamed. "I'm just saying I'm not ready to make any commitments."

Mom dropped her chin and stared him down. "I never asked your father to give up his dreams. Not once." She arched an eyebrow at Dad. "Did I?"

Dad touched her cheek, his gaze soft and loving. "Nope. If I remember correctly, your exact words were, 'When you're ready to let go of your wild ways and want to settle down, you come find me.'"

Mom turned her cheek into his palm. "And it took all of three days before you came knocking on my door."

"Hey, it was tough deciding between life on the road doing the circuit or marrying the most beautiful, loving and kindhearted woman I'd ever met. And I don't look at it as giving up my dreams but changing my dreams."

Mom laughed softly. "You made a wise choice."

Dad took her hand and lifted it to his lips. "I did. I've never regretted a day of my life since you've been a part of it. You gave me the greatest gifts. Your love and Nick and Cody."

Tears flowed down Mom's cheeks.

Seeing his parents' obvious love for each other constricted the muscles in Nick's throat. A deep longing welled from within Nick, making him glad he was seated. He wanted a love like his parents had. A love that would last through happiness and sorrow.

But was he ready for it? Could he sacrifice his dreams to embrace love? Was there a way to have both? He just didn't know.

After a tearful goodbye and promises to keep them informed on any developments, Nick and Ted left his parents' house in Marshal's Jeep, since Gordon had taken Frank and Lee up the mountain again. They were practicing while Nick's life was unraveling around him. They didn't know how good they had it.

At the television station, Nick asked for Julie. Her boss, Liam, came out of his office and shook his hand. Liam was tall, imposing and direct. "Julie went to the urgent care. She had an accident this morning."

Panic rioted within his chest. "She's hurt?"

"Her wrist. She fell down some stairs."

Needing to see that she was okay for himself, Nick left the station. Ted drove him to the urgent care. They found her and Bob signing out.

Her right wrist was wrapped in an ACE bandage and a half cast. She gave him a lopsided smile when she saw him. Her face was pale and her eyes filled with pain.

"What happened?" Nick asked.

"It was an accident," she said. "Kitty and I were talking—"

He reared back. "Kitty? She did this to you?"

"No," Julie said. "She was upset and her purse knocked into me. I lost my balance."

Bob stepped to Julie's side. "The intern who witnessed the incident said it looked deliberate."

A fierce anger roared through Nick's blood. He hated seeing Julie hurt. Hated worse that he'd brought this on her by allowing Kitty access to her. He should have made it clear to Kitty a long time ago that her attention was unwanted. He'd naively hoped her obsession would fade. Instead, Kitty's fixation had injured the person he loved.

He staggered back a step. His heart flooded with emotion until he thought his ribs would pop apart.

To cover his reaction, he backed up another step. "I'll deal with Kitty."

He whirled away and retreated, but the realization wouldn't be so easily dismissed. He loved Julie. With a love so fierce and strong he could barely breathe.

He needed air. He hit the door and stumbled outside. He braced his hands on his knees and bent over, gulping in huge amounts of oxygen, but he couldn't seem to get enough.

"Mr. Walsh, you okay?"

Not about to admit to having a panic attack over the fact that he loved Julie, he straightened and pulled the edges of his control together. "Yes. I have some long overdue business with Kitty Rogers."

He jammed his hand inside the breast pocket of his jacket. When he'd left the hospital after his crash, he'd stuffed the note and money clip Kitty had given him into the pocket. He unfolded the note. Staring at the neat script, he said, "We're going to the TownePlace Suites to talk to Kitty."

Not far from the Old Mill shopping district where the aerial competition had been held, the extended-stay hotel had a good view of the Deschutes River. Kitty's suite was on the ground floor in the southwest corner. A blue truck was parked outside the front door. Nick pounded on the door. From inside, he could hear voices. Then the canned laughter of a television.

"Kitty, open up!"

The door was flung partway open. A tall, lanky man stood in the open doorway. Beyond him Nick could see a kitchenette, a living room and dining area.

"You." Dark eyes regarded Nick with hostility. "What do you want?"

Nick was sure he'd never met this man. Was this Kitty's brother? "I need to talk to Kitty. Is she here?"

The man's gaze flicked to Ted and back. "Not yet. She should be here soon." He stepped back. "Come on in. You can wait for her." The man walked away, leaving the door partially open.

Nick stepped forward, but Ted's hand on his shoulder stopped him.

"Let me," Ted said.

With his hand on the weapon holstered at his side, Ted walked inside, passing a table with a large blue-and-white vase filled with flowers. Nick followed, leaving the door open. Ted stopped. Nick stepped past him and looked around. The suite looked like many others he'd stayed in over the years as he traveled from one competition to another. Nondescript, impersonal. Lonely.

He shook his thoughts away and focused on the man sitting on the couch with his legs stretched out and his arms splayed across the back of the couch.

"Who are you?" Nick asked.

His mouth stretched in a feral smile. His gaze flicked past Nick for a second, then zeroed back on him. Unease slide down Nick's spine.

"Your worst nightmare."

Before Nick could process that remark, a loud crash from his left sent his heart lurching. Blue-and-white shards of ceramic rained down as Ted crumpled to the floor in a heap. A hard shove in the middle of Nick's back sent him sprawling forward onto his hands and knees. He heard the sound of running feet as the unseen assailant escaped out the open door.

The guy on the couch leaped to his feet, producing a rifle he'd had hidden on the couch. Lifting his head, Nick found himself staring into the dark and menacing barrel of the rifle.

"Get up!" the guy demanded.

Nick's gaze swung to Ted. He lay unconscious on the floor. A gash on the back of his head bled bright red. Concern lanced Nick. He sent up a silent prayer that Ted wasn't dead.

"I said get up." The barrel jammed into Nick's shoulder.

Nick's pulse jumped. "You're the one who's been trying to kill me." He got to his feet, his hands raised in supplication. "Why are doing this? Who are you?"

"Never you mind," the guy said. "Turn around."

Flushing with rage, Nick said, "No. If you're going to shoot me, you're going to have to face me."

"I'm not gonna shoot you," he said. "I have something else in mind. We're going for a ride."

Caution tripped over him. He planted his feet wide. "I'm not going anywhere with you."

"Yes, you will, if you want your girlfriend to live," the guy said. "We're walking out the front door and getting into the truck right outside."

"Kitty is not my girlfriend," Nick shot back.

He snorted. "I'm talking about the blonde reporter. Kitty says you have a thing going with her."

Fear punched Nick in the gut, stealing his breath. "You leave her out of this."

"Gladly, as long as you cooperate." Keeping the rifle aimed at Nick's heart, he gestured to a black bag sitting on the kitchenette counter. "Open that bag. Use the plastic zip ties and bind your wrists together."

Figuring it was better to go and wait for

an opportunity to get the upper hand than get shot in the chest, Nick did as instructed. Using the zip ties, he bound his wrists.

"Make 'em tight," the guy barked.

Nick tugged, making a show of pulling them tighter but not really applying much pressure. "At least tell me your name."

"Troy. My name's Troy." Using the barrel, he nudged Nick. "Now outside, to the truck.

"Why are you doing this, Troy?"

"Stop talking, just move. There's a mountain waiting for us."

"Nick's not answering his cell phone or the phone at Marshal's house," Julie said to Bob. They were back at the station in the editing room. Bob had wanted to show her the footage they had so far on Nick. But she couldn't concentrate on work. She'd called Nick and left several messages, asking him to contact her. She wasn't sure what he was doing or what he meant when he'd said he'd take care of Kitty. But she had an edgy feeling in the pit of her stomach that wouldn't go away.

"He's fine. He's a big boy, he can take care of himself," Bob said. "Besides, he has his babysitter with him."

Julie slanted him an irritated glance. "Bodyguard," she corrected. "And the reason he has a bodyguard is someone is trying to kill him."

"All the more reason for you to stay away from him," Bob stated with a reproachful stare. "Ever since he came into town, he's put your life in danger."

"It's not his fault."

Bob rolled his eyes. "Yeah, well, I don't see what's so great about Nick Walsh."

Everything. There was so much about Nick that she admired. His kindness, his loyalty and his perseverance. She liked the way he focused on her when they were together, making it clear that she had his attention despite the chaos going on in his life. She enjoyed spending time with him, enjoyed his sense of humor and his strength of character. Over the past few days, she'd come to realize he wasn't nearly the adrenaline junkie she'd at first thought. Yes, he did amazing aerial jumps that took her breath away and skied like a maniac down a mountain, but he was grounded and trustworthy.

The type of guy who made her heart pound and her blood race.

She'd miss him when he left town.

Aware of Bob's probing gaze, she said, "I'm going to get coffee. Do you want some?"

"You're in love with him, aren't you?" Bob said, his voice low and intense.

"What?" She tried to dismiss his words with a forced laugh even as heat flushed through her cheeks. "No, no. Of course not."

Bob shook his head, but his dubious expression was easy to read. He didn't believe her. And frankly, neither did she.

The truth was she had fallen for Nick. But she could never let Nick know. Her life was here, his was off traveling the world competing, always looking for the perfect jump, the next big win. Next month he'd be competing in another country, jumping for the top prize. And in four more years, despite his talk of being too old, he'd be doing it again, in a different country but still chasing the same prize. She could never ask him to give that up.

"Hey, Julie." Bryce practically ran into the room. "She's back! Should I call the police?"

Surprise washed through her. "Do you mean Kitty?"

"Yes. She's at your desk. I didn't know what I should do," Bryce said.

Bob stood. "I'll take care of this."

Julie stayed him with a hand. "No. I'll talk to her."

Hopefully she'd know where Nick was.

Julie left the conference room and headed to her desk. Behind him, Bryce and Bob followed a few feet away. Julie appreciated their protectiveness. She approached Kitty, noticing the way her hands rubbed together and the pinched look on her face.

"Kitty, what do you want?"

She jumped up. "Ms. Frost, I'm so sorry for earlier. I really didn't mean to knock you down the stairs with my purse."

Kitty's contrition appeared sincere. Compassion and absolution rose within Julie. "I know. You're forgiven."

Kitty's shoulders visibly relaxed. "Oh, good. Thank you. I'd hate anyone to think I could deliberately hurt someone."

Which was exactly what Julie had been wondering. Her belief that Kitty was genuinely contrite wavered. Was Kitty behind the attempts on Nick's life? "Have you seen Nick since this morning?"

Kitty shook her head. A fat tear welled and slipped down one cheek. "No. I figured when he heard about your accident that he'd think I did it on purpose." Her dark eyes begged for Julie to understand. "Please don't tell Nick."

"He already knows. He came to the urgent care and saw what happened. Then he took off. He went to your hotel to talk to you. I guess he missed you," Julie said.

Kitty went still. "He what? He went to the hotel where I'm staying?" She grimaced. "That's not good. Troy will be upset."

"Troy?" The name echoed in Julie's head. "Troy, the one who designed your business logo?"

"He's a family friend. He insisted on driving me out here. He's good company most of the time."

"Why would Troy be upset?" Julie asked, concerned by the thought of Nick walking into something unexpected, like Kitty's male friend.

"Oh, he's got it in his silly head that we're meant to be together, despite the fact that my heart belongs to Nick."

Anxiety knocked against Julie's ribs. "Could Troy be the one who's been trying to kill Nick?"

Kitty pulled a face. "Oh, no. Troy wouldn't do anything like that. He's the sweetest guy ever. So patient and kind."

"Even with someone he sees as a threat to his happiness?"

"Threat to his…" Kitty waved away her words. "No, he understands. We're just traveling companions. We always get a two-room suite so we each have our own space. He'd never get in a fistfight. He might yell and thump around, but he's harmless."

"Can you call Troy and ask if he's seen Nick?" Julie asked, praying Nick was safe at Marshal's house already.

Kitty took her cell phone from her purse and dialed. It rang and rang. When the voice mail picked up, Julie's unease ratcheted a knot.

"Call the hotel and have them call the room," Julie prodded.

The hotel room's landline wasn't picked up, either.

"He's probably off exploring," Kitty said. "He does that a lot. Or he could be in the shower. Or asleep."

"Let's go to your suite." Julie needed to find Nick and make sure he was safe.

"We can if you'll drive," Kitty said. "I don't have a car. And since I can't get a hold of Troy, I'm stuck in town until he calls back. He has the truck we drove out here in."

"I'm okay with driving," Julie said and hustled Kitty out of the television station to the compact sedan Marshal had lent her as she waited for her car to be returned with a new tire.

Kitty slid into the passenger seat. "Nice leather."

Julie nodded, her throat too tight to answer. She needed to know Nick was okay. She drove them to the TownePlace, one of Bend's more upscale hotels. Julie had never stayed in any of the suites, but she'd eaten in the hotel's restaurant, which was superb.

Now, the last thing on her mind was food. She followed Kitty to the door of her suite. It was closed and locked. Kitty used her card key to enter, then let out a startled yelp.

Julie walked inside and stopped short. Ted lay unconscious on the floor, surrounded by broken chunks of pottery. She rushed to his side, checked his neck for a pulse and breathed out a sigh of relief to feel a strong, steady beat. Where was Nick?

"Kitty, call 9-1-1," Julie demanded. A deep panic built in her chest. Ted was hurt and Nick was nowhere in sight. What had Troy done with him? Was Nick still alive? Would they find him before it was too late?

Julie sent up a prayer. *Please, Lord, protect Nick.*

# FOURTEEN

"Why are you doing this? What have I done to you?" Nick asked Troy.

They were in an older-model truck, chugging along a back road to Mt. Bachelor. The inside of the cab smelled like stale tobacco and beer. Empty cans and chew pouches littered the floor. Nick kicked them aside and planted his feet on the floor as the truck slipped on icy patches on the snow packed road. Outside, the afternoon sun started its descent, elongating the shadows of the huge ponderosa pines and Douglas firs making up the Deschutes National Forest. Cloud cover had rolled in, threatening another deluge of snow within the next several hours. The temperature had dropped, and without the heater on a chill crept through Nick's jacket and prickled his skin.

"Besides stealing Kitty's heart?" Troy slanted him a harsh glare. "Nothing."

Nick groaned. "I didn't steal Kitty's heart.

She's delusional. There is nothing going on between us."

"So you say." Troy's wide shoulders lifted and fell in a jerky motion. "But with you out of the way, she'll finally realize what she has in me. She won't need to follow you like some lost puppy anymore. Stitching your name in hats and buying you gifts."

"You put the spiders in the hats?"

"Nice touch, huh? Too bad they didn't get you."

Nick lifted his hands bound with a plastic zip tie, his palms up. "Hey, man, I'm all for stopping Kitty following me and buying me gifts. I'll help you any way I can. But you have to let me go."

Troy grinned, showing yellowed and stained teeth. "Naw. I've got too much riding on this now."

Frustrated, Nick strove to keep his voice even. "What do you hope to accomplish?"

"Accomplish?" Troy asked with a smirk. "Yeah, that's a good word. I'm gonna accomplish a feat that I've been working at for the past few months."

"Since cutting the brakes on my car and then loosening the binding on my ski didn't work."

Troy shrugged noncommittally.

"Did you take that photo of me at the doctor's office and deliver it to Julie? To the newspaper?"

"I delivered it, but I didn't take it."

Nick tried to digest that as another thought slammed into him. He swallowed back the bile rising to clog his throat. "Are you the one who killed Cody?"

Troy gave a negative shake of his head. "I had nothing to do with your brother's death. I didn't come on board until later. So you can't pin that on me."

Nick grappled to comprehend the information bombarding his mind. "You came on board?"

"Yep. The plan was to just injure you, but I figured if I'm gonna do it, I might as well do it all the way."

"Plan? Someone hired you to hurt me?"

Troy's jaw clenched.

"Who?" Nick pressed. "Who wants me dead?"

"I ain't saying another word," Troy muttered. "If I do, I won't be paid. I need that money. I got to impress Kitty. She's got to see I can take care of her. She needs me."

The guy was off his rocker. Nick felt as if he'd stepped into some bad horror flick.

As the parking lot for the ski resort came

into view, Nick kept an alert eye for a way to escape. Troy couldn't very well walk in plain view with the rifle, so as soon as they parked, Nick planned on jumping out. With his hands bound, he wouldn't be much in a fistfight, but no doubt he could outrun the lumbering man.

Troy parked the truck in the farthest slot away from the majority of vehicles then slid the rifle under the bench seat.

Nick took advantage of the moment to grab the silver door handle and tugged hard. The door popped open. He swung his legs out the door as something hard was jammed into his left side. He froze.

"Oh, no, you don't," Troy said, his voice deadly quiet.

Nick turned to see that Troy had traded his rifle for a handgun.

The sour taste of dread filled Nick's mouth.

"Climb out nice and easy or you'll get a bullet in the kidney." Troy nudged with the gun. Nick stood as Troy scooted over the bench to follow him out the passenger door.

When they were out, Troy moved to stand in front of Nick. The dark, menacing expression on the other man's face sent icy fingers of apprehension down Nick's back. Troy yanked the sleeves of Nick's jacket down over the zip tie, keeping his hands together.

"This is what we're doing," Troy said, his voice low and hard. "You're gonna walk nice and slow to the nearest chairlift. We're gonna get on. If you cooperate, no one else is gonna get hurt." Troy gestured, shoving the gun into Nick's belly. "But if you try to make a break for it, I'll start shooting. If I get you, great, but I might get some innocent kid. You don't want an innocent kid's blood on your head, do you?"

Nick ground his back teeth. Rage boiled in his blood. His gaze swept the parking lot, the path and the lift. Everywhere he looked, there were potential victims. Children, teens, women and men. None of whom deserved the wrath of this psycho. "You'll never get away with this."

"We'll see." Troy's lips thinned. "Let's go."

Making the agonizing trek to the Pine Marten chairlift, Nick tried to coax more information out of Troy. "Who's paying you to do this?"

"Never you mind," Troy stated, keeping the business end of the gun rammed into Nick's side.

The possibilities of who and why weighed on Nick's mind. "Is it a competitor? Someone I know? Or someone from a foreign nation?"

"I'm not saying nothing. Now stop your

jibber-jabbering. You're making me nervous," Troy said. "I get twitchy fingers when I'm nervous."

"We wouldn't want that," Nick grumbled. Snow clung to his leather boots. Cold air mingled with his breath, making a cloud. Without headgear for warmth, Nick's ears were going numb. He glanced at Troy. The guy must be impervious to the cold.

They got in line for the chairlift. It wasn't unusual for nonskiers to take the lift to the midmountain lodge for dinner in the gourmet restaurant, which had breathtaking views at seventy-eight hundred feet. People often came to watch the sunset while dining on fabulous cuisine. Nick didn't have any illusions as he and Troy positioned themselves to catch the lift—they weren't heading to the lodge for dinner reservations. Nick wasn't quite sure what Troy's plan was, but Nick assumed it had something to do with him not coming back down the mountain.

Troy flashed two lift tickets he'd obviously bought at some other time at the lift operator. The lift hit Nick behind the knees. With his hands bound he couldn't easily grab the middle pole without twisting slightly. He leaned back as the chair swooped him up above the ground, taking them up the mountain. Troy wrapped an arm around the pole. From the greenish look on his face, Nick guessed he didn't like heights.

Interesting. Nick could use that to his advantage. Gripping the chair with his legs, he rocked forward. The chair swung, tipping down slightly.

"Hey! Knock it off," Troy yelled and reached for the safety bar.

Nick raised his elbow, blocking the bar from coming down over their heads.

The distant sounds of sirens reached Nick. He prayed that meant help was on the way. He just needed to stay alive long enough for their help to matter.

With a groan of frustration and keeping a tight hold on the pole, Troy tucked the gun in the waistband of his jeans and then reached inside his front pants pocket for a pocketknife.

"Really?" Nick said eyeing the three-inch blade. "You're going kill me with your pocketknife?"

"Give me your hands," Troy barked out.

"I don't think anyone would believe I cut my wrists," Nick stated dryly.

"Just do it," Troy demanded.

Warily, Nick held out his bound wrists. He wasn't sure what to expect. When Troy cut the zip tie, surprise washed over Nick. Rubbing his wrists, he said, "Thanks."

"Don't thank me yet," Troy said and shoved Nick hard.

Careening precariously close to slipping off the chair, Nick gripped harder with his legs and grasped the side rail. Troy pummeled Nick, pushing and shoving, trying to loosen his hold on the rail.

Once Nick regained his equilibrium, he reacted swiftly, hooking the foot closest to Troy around Troy's calf and tugging while at the same time swinging his elbow, connecting with Troy's nose.

*"Awwwww!"* Troy yelled, releasing his hold on the middle pole to grab his bleeding nose.

Taking advantage of the moment, Nick tipped the chair forward, sending Troy flying out of the chair. Troy screamed on his way down. He face-planted in a deep drift; only the outline of his body where he'd sunk in the snow could be seen.

Nick sat back, letting the adrenaline drain through him to be replaced by relief.

It'd been a long time since Nick had had a shoving match on a chairlift. He and Cody used to grapple like a couple of boxers on the lifts, trying to get the other to fall off. They' each managed to unseat the other once. Neither had gotten seriously hurt. Cody had dislocated his shoulder. Nick had cracked a rib. Then their father had found out what they'd been up to and threatened to ban them from skiing if it happened again.

Nick had never imagined those wild antics with his brother would one day save his life.

Unfortunately, Nick wasn't out of the woods yet. There was still the person paying Troy. Nick had to find out who that was and stop him before he could celebrate his freedom.

At the top of the lift, he used the operator's phone to call the police and tell them where they could find Troy. He also told them about Ted and was informed his bodyguard was alive and in the hospital, recovering from a head wound. Relieved that Ted wasn't dead, Nick hung up. Then he took the lift back down the mountain, passing over the spot where Troy was being dug out of the snow by the ski patrol and the Bend police.

When Nick reached the bottom of the lift, Julie was there, bundled up in her red wool coat, a white hat jauntily perched on her head and her blond braid falling over her shoulder. His heart barrel-rolled in his chest. Elation at seeing her pretty face, her eyes so full of concern and relief, made him hurry to her. He gathered her close and hung on for all he was worth.

"I was so scared," she whispered. She pulled back to look at him. "Thank You, God, you're alive and in one piece. What happened?"

"I'm fine now that I'm with you," he said. He never wanted to let her go. He dipped his head and captured her soft, sweet lips in a heady kiss that stole his breath and left his senses spinning. He wanted to unbraid her hair and feel the soft ends sliding through his fingers. He wanted to pick her up and carry her off, like some medieval barbarian, claiming his woman.

The clearing of a throat jolted through the haze clouding Nick's mind. Julie eased back. He followed, unwilling to release her.

"Mr. Walsh," Detective Agee said, his voice insistent.

Frustrated, Nick broke the kiss. For a second he rested his forehead against Julie's. Then he straightened, tucking Julie into his side, his arm around her, his hand resting lightly on her hip. "Yes, Detective."

"I'm sorry to break this up," the detective said with a twinkle in his brown eyes. "But we need you to come to the station to take your statement."

"I understand. Julie's coming with me," Nick said, not willing to let her out of his sight. "There's something you should know. Troy was being paid. There's someone else out there who wants me dead."

Julie sat on the hard plastic chair in the Bend police station's waiting area. Her lips still tingled with the lingering memory of Nick's ardent kiss. She'd thought her heart would burst from her chest when he stepped off the lift in one piece. Ever since Ted awoke and said some guy with a gun had Nick, fear had camped out on her chest like a three hundred pound baby elephant, making it difficult to take a full breath. Thankfully, the hotel maid had seen Nick and Troy getting into an old truck. The police had put out an alert and found the truck parked at Mt. Bachelor.

Riding in the back of a police cruiser with Nick had been surreal. If Nick hadn't held her tightly to his side, she'd have been a bit freaked out. The metal grating separating the front and back and the locking doors had made her feel uncomfortable this time. She hoped she never had to ride in the back of a police car again.

When they arrived at the police station, Nick had been escorted to an interview room.

Troy had been arrested. He'd survived the fall and suffered only a broken arm. The drift he'd plunged into had saved him from a deadly landing.

Kitty had been detained after they found Ted unconscious in her hotel room. But she'd been released and now paced in front of Julie like a caged cat. Julie wasn't sure if Kitty was upset about Nick or Troy. Julie suspected Kitty wasn't sure herself.

"How long do you think they'll keep him?" Kitty asked, wringing her hands. "I have to know he's really okay."

"Who?" Julie asked. "Who are you worried about?"

"Troy. Nick." She grimaced, and tears filled her eyes. "Both of them."

Just as Julie thought. "Nick's fine. Troy's in a lot of trouble."

"I know." Kitty plopped down on a chair. "I don't understand why he wanted to hurt Nick."

"Don't you?" Julie said, wondering if Kitty's denseness was an act. "The guy loves you, Kitty." At least according to what Nick had told her on the trip down the mountain. "Someone was paying him money to hurt Nick. Do you have any idea who that could be?"

Kitty shook her head. "No." She leaned her head back against the wall. "It's so unbelievable."

"You really had no idea Troy was behind the attempts on Nick's life?" Julie found that hard to believe.

Kitty jumped up. "I didn't!"

Julie shrugged, not sure what to think.

"I need coffee." Kitty stalked away.

"Julie!" Gordon came charging into the waiting area, followed by Frank and Lee. "How's Nick? Where is he? Can I see him? Tell me he's not hurt!"

Julie held up a hand. "Whoa. He's fine. He's in giving his statement right now. He'll be out soon, I would expect."

"My phone was off so I didn't get the message that he was in trouble until just a bit ago," Gordon said.

"We heard Nick pushed someone off the chairlift," Frank said, rocking back on his heels.

"Only because the guy tried to knock him off," Julie retorted hotly.

"Good for Nick," Lee said. "What's the guy saying? Did he give a reason?"

"He lawyered up as soon as they set his arm."

"That's too bad," Lee said.

"He did tell Nick that he was being paid to try to hurt him."

Lee frowned. "By who?"

Frank whipped off the baseball cap perched on his head and ran a hand through his shaggy blond hair. "Man, that stinks. Who'd want Nick dead?"

"There's got to be a money trail," Gordon said. "There's always a money trail. I'm going to see what's going on." He walked away and disappeared down the hall.

"Uh-oh, crazy alert," Frank said, gesturing with his head toward Kitty as she approached at a fast clip.

Lee nudged him. "Behave."

Kitty skidded to a halt in front of Lee and Frank. "Did you hear? Troy tried to kill Nick."

Julie looked at the pair of skiers. "You two know Troy?"

Lee shrugged. "He's around all the time."

"Like she is," Frank added, gesturing with his thumb at Kitty.

Kitty made a face at Frank.

"How come Nick had never met him?" Julie asked.

"'Cause Nick's above hanging out with the fringe crowd," Frank replied. "He's not into the after-parties anymore."

"What should I do?" Kitty said, her gaze on Lee. "How do I help Troy?"

Lee's eyes hardened. "The man tried to kill my friend and you want me to tell you how to help him?"

Hurt clouded Kitty's dark eyes. "Troy's your friend, too."

Something scary flashed in Lee's eyes. "Kitty, you need to hire a lawyer."

"But I—"

Lee stood abruptly and gripped Kitty by the elbow, tugging her away. They stopped out of earshot of where Julie sat.

Curious situation that Lee and Troy had been friends and Nick didn't know about the friendship. Julie would make sure to mention the connection to Nick.

Frank adjusted his ball cap, drawing her attention. "She's bad news."

As she stared at the logo on the ball cap, Julie's pulse sped up. Now that she'd really looked at the hat, it seemed familiar. She racked her brain trying to recall where she'd seen it before. Then it came to her. The man who'd delivered the photo of Nick to the television had been wearing the same hat with the same strange design.

Something Gordon had said that first night played in Julie's head.

*"There are thirteen guys from the B and C teams ready and willing to step into his place on the A team, including the two skiers who were just here. And more behind them that would jump at the chance to be invited to join the U.S. ski team."*

Was Frank the man behind the attempts on Nick's life?

Considering how resentful the younger skier had been acting, it wasn't a stretch.

Needing to tread carefully, she said, "Interesting hat."

Frank touched the brim. "It's broken-in nice, the way I like it."

"Where did you get it?"

He thought for a moment. "It's actually Lee's. He got it from the vendor at some ski trade show last year."

Her heart thudded. "The hat belongs to Lee?"

"Yep, but he said he didn't want it anymore, so he gave it to me."

Swallowing the trepidation clogging her throat, her gaze slid to where Lee and Kitty were deep in conversation. Julie turned to Frank and asked, "When did he give it to you?"

"This morning." Frank's hazel eyes were curious. "What's with the questions?"

Her gaze strayed back to Lee and Kitty in time to see Kitty walk out the front door. Lee met her gaze, his brown eyes flat and sending a shiver of apprehension down her spine.

"Nothing." She jumped to her feet. "I'm going to check on Nick."

Hurrying toward the sergeant's desk, she intended to tell Detective Agee what she suspected—that Lee was the person behind the attempts on Nick's life.

"Excuse me," she said trying to get someone's attention. Everyone seemed to be busy either on the phone or with someone.

"I'll be with you in a moment," the sergeant called from across the squad room.

"Julie, is something wrong?" Lee's voice near her shoulder sent a chill across her flesh.

She whipped around and stepped back. "No, why would you ask that?" Her tone ended on a high note.

"You look a little sick." He cupped her elbow. "Let's get you some air."

"That's okay." She dug in her heels. "I don't need to go outside."

His grip tightened and something sharp poked into her side. "Don't make this difficult. If you scream, I'll shove this knife all the way in." His flinty eyes regarded her coldly. "Let's go."

"No!" She opened her mouth to let loose a scream.

The tip of the knife jabbed harder into her flesh. She doubled over on a yelp as unbearable pain sluiced through her.

Lee wrapped an arm around her and propelled her out of the police station, into the dark.

A fierce anger swamped Julie. A man Nick thought of as a brother was actually his worst enemy.

# FIFTEEN

Nick walked out of the police interview room, glad to have that part of this ordeal over with. He'd repeated his conversation with Troy at least three times. Each time one of the three detectives would want some detail filled in, like was Troy left-or right-handed. As if Nick had paid attention.

Detective Agee stepped out of another room and handed him his cell phone. "We found this in Mr. MacAfee's truck."

Palming the device, Nick tucked it into his jacket pocket. "Thanks."

"How are you holding up?"

"Better now that Troy is in custody," Nick said, falling into step with the detective. "Has Troy said who's paying him?"

"No. Mr. MacAfee has gone silent, waiting for a lawyer. Supposedly Ms. Rogers is hiring one."

"Of course she is," Nick grumbled. "Did

they find his weapon?" Nick hated to think what would happen if some kid or teenager happened upon the handgun.

"Yes, it was recovered. A nice piece. A .38 Special," Agee said. "We also secured the .223 rifle from the truck under the seat, like you said."

"What happens now?" Nick asked as they stopped at the desk sergeant's station.

"Mr. MacAfee will have his due process. He's facing charges of kidnapping, attempted murder and assault. If we can tie him to your brother's fatality, then murder, as well."

"He claimed he wasn't involved in Cody's death." But whoever hired Troy had orchestrated Cody's demise in an attempt to hurt him. Anger at the unknown person responsible twisted in Nick's chest like a corkscrew, driving deep into his heart. "Do you think Troy will give up who he's working for?"

"Only time will tell," Agee said. "We're following every lead we can."

"There you are!" Gordon hurried down the hall and stopped beside Nick. Concern etched lines in his otherwise smooth face. "You okay? Are you injured?"

Nick placed his hand on his manager's shoulder. "No worse for the wear."

Gordon heaved a relieved sigh. "Great.

I've been fielding calls. The press got wind of your abduction and then the committee called wanting reassurances that you were still ready and able to compete."

"You're doing a great job," Nick said, squeezing his shoulder. "Where's Julie?"

"Last I saw her she and the guys were in the waiting area," Gordon replied.

Nick turned to the detective. "Is there anything else you need from me?"

"Not at this time. I'll be in touch if there are developments," Agee said and walked away.

With purposeful strides, Nick headed toward the waiting area. He wanted to see Julie, hold her and kiss her. He needed to tell her what was in his heart. That he'd fallen deeply, madly in love with her.

But what good would come of that? A voice in his head mocked.

Her life was in Bend, while he still had so much to do before he relinquished his goals because he happened to have fallen in love with a woman. Did he really expect her to wait for him? To give up her dream of hosting *Northwest Edition* to follow him to the other side of the world?

His steps slowed. He wiped his sweating palms on his thighs. Nerves revved in his blood. Anguish squeezed his heart in a vise-like grip.

No, he couldn't tell Julie that he loved her. Not until… He stopped as thoughts bombarded him. Plans formulated. Options ran rampant. The future opened up in his mind like a vast and wondrous view from the tip of the mountain.

Gordon ran into him. "What's wrong?"

Suddenly everything solidified and came together to form a coherent idea. For the first time in his life, winning wasn't the foremost desire in his heart and his mind. He wanted to marry Julie, live his life here in the place he grew up. He wanted to spend his days helping others learn the sport he loved while he spent his nights with the woman he loved.

Now he just had to figure out if Julie felt the same. He sent up a silent plea, asking God for guidance.

He clapped Gordon on the back. "Nothing. Nothing is wrong."

Nick hurried forward, anxious to see Julie. When he rounded the corner, only Frank sat on one of the hard plastic chairs. "Where's Julie?" Nick asked.

Frank rose and came forward holding out his hand. "Hey, glad you're okay."

Shaking his hand, Nick said, "Yeah, me, too." Then he repeated his question. "Where's Julie?"

Frank shrugged. "Lee took her outside. She must not have been feeling well, 'cause she was doubled over like she had a stomach bug or something."

Concerned arched through Nick. He started to turn toward the exit when something registered in his mind. He whirled back to stare at the hat tipped back on Frank's head. Pointing to the blue baseball cap, Nick asked, "Where'd you get that?"

Frank whipped off the hat. "What's with all the questions about this wretched hat? First Julie, now you? It was Lee's, okay? He gave it to me."

A fissure of panic blasted through Nick's being like a physical blow. He recognized the hat from the video he'd watched at the television station. Obviously Julie had as well. Nick's mind tried to wrap around the idea that Lee could be the person who'd dropped off the offending photo. But why?

The reason slammed into Nick with the force of an out-of-control semi coming down the pass. Lee wanted Nick's spot on the team traveling to the biggest sporting event in the world. And Lee was willing to kill for the opportunity to compete for gold. Nick wanted to give his friend, the man he had thought of as a brother, the benefit of the doubt, but the sentiment wouldn't come. The certainty embedded itself so far in that Nick knew he'd have a scar from the betrayal.

But would Lee go so far as to hurt Julie?

"We need to find them," Nick said. He quickly explained to Gordon what he was thinking.

"No way, man," Frank stated. "Lee's a good guy. He wouldn't do that."

The grim set to Gordon's mouth let Nick know Gordon believed Lee capable of such treachery.

"You tell Detective Agee," Nick instructed Gordon. "I'm going to find them. I'll keep my cell on."

Nick ran for the door.

"Wait for me," Frank yelled and raced to catch up.

Outside the police station, Nick scanned the parking lot. "How did you and Lee get here?"

"Marshal's Jeep, but it's gone," Frank stated glumly. "Man, I can't believe this."

"Where would he take her?" Nick asked

aloud, his mind sifting through possible places Lee would go. The only place Nick could think of was the motor home. The fumes from the exterminator had to be gone by now. But to what end? What did Lee hope to accomplish by kidnapping Julie? What did he plan to do with her? To her?

Dread clawed at him. If Lee hurt her… A smoldering rage filled Nick. His fingers curled into fists. He'd never thought of himself as a violent man, but he wanted to smash his fist into Lee's face.

Nick's cell phone rang. He dug it out of the pocket of his jacket. The caller ID sent his heart booming. Lee.

Nick depressed the answer button and the speaker button. "You better not hurt her."

Lee tsked. "Slow down, man. I won't touch a hair on her pretty head as long as you co-operate."

Frank's jaw dropped open. He shook his head at the proof his friend wasn't the good guy he'd thought he was.

"Cooperate?" Nick said, trying hard to keep from yelling. "What do you want?"

"No police. Come alone to the RV. Don't tell anyone, especially not Frank," Lee said. "He'd open his mouth for sure."

Nick quickly took the call off speaker as Frank sputtered in anger.

"I'll come, but you do anything to her and—"

"And what?" Lee barked out a short laugh. "You're such a gaper."

Nick rolled his eyes at Lee's use of the term, signifying Lee thought Nick was completely clueless.

"You wouldn't know what to do," Lee continued. "Mr. Golden Boy had it so good his whole life. Some of us had to scrape and scrabble to get here."

"That's what this is about? Poor you and your awful upbringing?" Nick's fingers clenched around the phone. "Let Julie go, Lee."

"I will. When you get here." Lee hung up.

Frank whipped off the baseball hat and threw it on the ground. "Man, I'm gonna bust his head for this."

"No, you're not. You're going inside and telling Detective Agee to get to the trailer."

Frank stared at him. "You're not going up to the mountain alone. How ya gonna get there?"

"Walk, if I have to." He spotted a car pulling into the parking lot. "Go tell Agee," Nick said and broke into a run. He skidded to a halt as an older man climbed out of the driver's side of the gold sedan. "Hey, I need to borrow your car. It's a matter of life and death!"

"What? Nick, you okay?" The man stared at Nick in confusion.

Nick did a double take. "Principal Andrews! Aw, sweet. Can I borrow your car?"

"Uh, sure."

"Thanks. Man, I love small towns." Nick snagged the keys dangling from the man's hand, slid into the driver's seat and slammed the door. He jammed the key in the ignition and started the car. In a spray of rock salt, snow and dirt, he stomped on the gas and sped out of the parking lot. He had to save Julie. Nothing else mattered. Not even winning gold.

Julie held her side where the tip of Lee's knife had sliced into skin. Thankfully, the cut was superficial, but the wound burned like crazy. She'd wedged herself into the corner of the dinette inside Nick's traveling motor home. Lee had allowed her to dress the wound with supplies from the motor home's first aid kit while he went to the front of the trailer to call Nick. She heard Lee's side of the conversation. Nick was smart; he'd know not to listen to Lee's directive to come alone.

They needed the police. It would be only a matter of time before help arrived. At least she prayed so.

Lee walked the few steps to stand directly in front of where she sat. He leaned a hip against the sink.

"What did you mean you had to scrape to get where you are?" she asked, hoping to keep him distracted so when the police and Nick showed up he wouldn't be prepared. Nick hadn't told her much about Lee's background. She hadn't thought to do research on Lee or Frank, because neither was the subject of her feature story.

Lee shrugged. "Doesn't matter."

"It does if it's what's motivating you. I'd like to know why you've kidnapped me. Why you stabbed me."

He winced. "Sorry about that, but I couldn't have you alerting anyone."

"You won't get away with this," she said. "You know that, right?"

Which didn't bode well for her safety since she and Nick could identify him. She suppressed a shiver of alarm. Once Lee had what he wanted, he would have no choice but to kill her and Nick, when Nick showed up. And Nick would show up. He wouldn't let anything happen to her. He was that kind of guy.

Honorable and loyal. Brave and true. A man worth pinning her heart on. She prayed she'd have a chance to tell him she loved him.

"All Nick has to do is withdraw from the competition and we'll all be happy," Lee stated. "I'll go in his place since I'm next in line. I almost had enough points to edge him out, but not quite."

The man was delusional if he thought he would be able to resume his life as if nothing had happened. Lee had paid Troy to have Nick killed. But Troy had said he wasn't around when Cody had died. Which meant...

Bile rose in Julie's throat as she met Lee's flat gaze. "You killed Cody!"

The sickening realization eclipsed the stinging in her side.

"That was a mistake," Lee protested. "It was Nick's water bottle. Cody wasn't supposed to drink from it."

"But he did and he died because of you," Julie said with disgust lacing her words.

"I didn't want to hurt Cody. He was like my little brother." Lee swiped the back of his hand across his mouth.

"What about Nick? Isn't he like a brother to you, too?"

Lee's lip curled. "Yeah. An annoying older brother. He gets everything handed to him.

The best sponsors, the best girls, the best scores. I'm better than him. I should be the one representing Thunderbird. Instead, I'm stuck with All Good Sports Drink. Their logo is a silly smiley face. Not cool. Not at all."

He sounded like a sullen teenager. "How did you connect with Troy?"

Lee scoffed. "That buffoon. He couldn't do anything right. All I wanted was Nick hurt. But he kept botching it."

"So instead you tried to kill Nick," Julie accused.

"No! That was Troy. I've only ever wanted Nick to get injured. It was Troy's idea to kill him. The guy was mad with jealousy over Kitty's infatuation with Nick. He was eager to get Nick out of the way."

That matched what Nick had related about Troy. "How much did you pay him?"

"Twenty grand up front." Lee rubbed his jaw. "Worst money I ever spent. I should have stuck with doing it myself, but I thought it would be a win-win. He'd get rid of the competition for Kitty's attention and I'd get rid of my competition. Not so much."

The sound of tires screeching to a halt outside the motor home jump-started Julie's pulse. Nick was here.

A moment later there was a pounding on the door.

"Lee!" Nick shouted. "Open this door. Where's Julie?"

Lee reached over and undid the lock. Nick yanked the door open and rushed up the stairs. Julie met his frantic gaze.

"You're hurt!" he exclaimed when his gaze shifted to the bloody mess of gauze on the table.

"A flesh wound, man," Lee said, flashing the long blade in his hand. "Don't get yourself all twisted up."

A muscle ticked in Nick's jaw. "You let her go. Now."

Julie had never heard Nick use such a cold, menacing tone before and it scared her nearly as much as Lee's knife.

Lee straightened to his full height, which put him an inch or so taller than Nick. "She's leverage. You have to do something for me first."

"No. I'm not doing anything for you," Nick growled and charged at Lee.

Julie yelped and scooted out of the way as the two men grappled for control of the knife. They crashed into the wall, then crashed onto the table, causing it to collapse beneath their weight. Nick landed on top of Lee. A loud roar of pain filled Julie's ears.

With one hand on her heart and the other over her mouth, she keened with dread. *Please, Lord, don't let Nick get hurt!*

Nick jumped to his feet and backed away. Lee lay immobile on the floor of the motor home, wedged between the sink and the remains of the table, the knife sticking out of his shoulder. Blood dripped from the wound. He moaned and his gaze grew cloudy with shock.

Julie scrambled off the bench seat and flew into Nick's embrace. He held her tight in his arms as shudders ran a violent course through her. "I thought you were… I was so afraid," she whispered, her voice breaking on a sob.

"Shh, it's okay," Nick soothed. "We're both safe."

Suddenly the motor home was crowded as police officers stormed in, their weapons drawn. After assessing the situation and determining the threat had been neutralized, they put their weapons away.

The lead officer gestured for them to move his way. "Folks, let's get you out of here so the paramedics can get in to treat him."

Reluctantly, Julie released her hold on Nick

and took the officer's hand. Stepping over Lee, she squeezed her way to the door.

"Hey!"

The shout jolted her heart and she whipped her gaze back to see Lee had grabbed Nick's foot as he tried to step over him.

"Let go, Lee. It's over. You're done."

"I'm sorry," Lee said. "So sorry."

Nick shook off Lee's hand and stepped in behind Julie. With his hand on her waist, he urged her out of the RV.

Once they hit the ground, they were pressed out of the way by the paramedics.

Nick wrapped his arms around her.

With her heart in her throat, she took his face in her hands and stared into his vivid blue eyes. The tenderness she saw shining there gave her the courage to confess, "I love you."

A crooked grin spread across his face. "I love you, too."

"Really?"

"Yes, really." He dipped his head and she rose on tiptoe to meet him in a blissful kiss full of promise.

She ignored the quiver of uncertainty trying to rob her of happiness. She didn't know how it would work out between them. They had separate lives. Hers was here, his everywhere else. But for now she'd revel in the love surrounding her.

The next day the sun shone bright, and the sky was a brilliant blue. Not a cloud in the sky. Snow covering Cody's grave glistened in the sunlight. Nick's heart filled with raw emotion. The memorial service had been a wonderful tribute to a life cut short. People had gathered to pay their respects. His mother had wept, but she'd also smiled.

Nick breathed in deeply of the fresh mountain air and sent a prayer of praise heavenward.

Praise that Cody's killer had been brought to justice. The press had reported the truth, repairing the damage they'd done to Cody's reputation. The stabbing guilt Nick felt had lessened to a tolerable level. He would always miss his baby brother. And he knew one day they would see each other again in Heaven.

It was still hard to believe Lee had been the one behind it all. Lee's wounded shoulder would heal and he'd be charged and would stand trial for his crimes. Nick felt bad for Frank, who was struggling with the betrayal as much as Nick. Frank had flown out this morning, returning to his home in Utah. He'd said he needed time.

They all needed time.

Julie stepped to Nick's side and slipped her slender hand in his. Another reason to send praise to God. Nick could hardly comprehend how blessed he was to have Julie's love.

But there was still so much they needed to work out before they could start their journey together.

"You're leaving today, aren't you?" she asked quietly.

Keeping his gaze on the mountain in the distance, he answered, "I have to get back to training. The committee will make their announcement in a few days."

"And you have to be ready to go compete in the biggest game of your life."

There was understanding in her tone. He ached to know what to say, what to do. He couldn't stay. Not yet. And he couldn't ask her to give up her chance at securing her promotion.

"Julie, I'm—"

She stepped in front of him, forcing him to meet her sparkling blue eyes. Tears glistened in the sunlight. "I know. You have to go. I want you to go."

Hurt pierced through his heart. "You do?"

"You have to go and win." She laid her

hand over his heart. "We'll deal with everything else after."

He covered her hand with his own, relieved to know her love was true. "Yes, we will. Because I'm coming back. I want to make my life here with you."

"You do?"

"I do."

"But what about competing?" Her voice quivered slightly.

"After this one last competition—" the competition of a lifetime "—I'm retiring. I want to coach."

"You'll be great at it." Her voice rang with confidence.

The burn of joyful tears made his voice gruff as love expanded in his chest. "What did I do to deserve you?"

She slipped her arms around him and laid her cheek on his chest. "We're blessed."

"Yes. Yes, we are." He kissed the top of her head as contentment filled his soul. "Whether I stand on the podium or not, I've already won."

Leaning back, she beamed up at him. "My champion."

\* \* \* \* \*

Dear Reader,

Thank you for going on this wild ride with Julie and Nick as they faced challenges, both personally and professionally, on the way to falling in love.

When my editor asked if I could come up with a story featuring a winter sport, I had a hard time deciding which sport to focus on. There are so many interesting ones! I chose to have Nick be an aerial freestyle skier because I love watching the sport. It's a fairly new addition to the many winter events that have captured the world. I found it fascinating to learn more about this exciting sporting event.

After watching several national and world championships and seeing the excitement of the reporters talking to the athletes, I decided to have my heroine be a fledging reporter. Julie was a fun character to develop as I researched the broadcasting field.

I hope you enjoyed this story as much as I enjoyed writing it.

May you be blessed,

## Questions for Discussion

1. What made you pick up this book to read? In what ways did it live up to your expectations?

2. In what ways were Julie and Nick realistic characters? How did their romance build believably? How did the suspense build?

3. What about the setting was clear and appealing?

4. As a professional skier, Nick faced many challenges on and off the slopes. What challenges do you face in your life that affects your work? Your family?

5. Julie had been betrayed in a relationship and that led her to pursue her career goals. What motivates you in your life goals?

6. Nick felt guilty for his brother's death, falsely believing he could have stopped the accident from happening. Can you share a time when you felt guilt for something that was out of your control?

7. Nick allowed guilt to put a wedge be-

tween himself and God. What kinds of things do you let in between you and your relationship with God?

8. Julie's relationship with her stepfather was strained. Why do you think that was?

9. Nick saw his parents' love and wanted that kind of love for himself. Can you give some examples of loving couples who have influenced your life?

10. Nick and Julie had grown up around each other. As they became acquainted with each other as adults, their perceptions of each other changed. Can you talk about how we change as we mature? In what ways have you changed?

11. At the end of the story, Nick decided to let go of his career to be with Julie. Have you ever sacrificed a goal or dream for someone you love? Please share the experience.

12. Did you notice the Scripture in the beginning of the book? What do you think God means by these words? What application does the Scripture have to your life?

13. How did the author's use of language/ writing style make this an enjoyable read?

14. Discuss whether you would or would not read more from this author.

15. What will be your most vivid memories of this book? What lessons about life, love and faith did you learn from this story?

# LARGER-PRINT BOOKS!

## GET 2 FREE LARGER-PRINT NOVELS PLUS 2 FREE MYSTERY GIFTS

*Love Inspired®*
## SUSPENSE
RIVETING INSPIRATIONAL ROMANCE

### Larger-print novels are now available...

LISLPDIR13R

# LARGER-PRINT BOOKS!

**GET 2 FREE
LARGER-PRINT NOVELS
PLUS 2 FREE
MYSTERY GIFTS**

*Love Inspired*

*Larger-print novels are now available...*

LILPDIRI

# ReaderService.com

## Manage your account online!

- Review your order history
- Manage your payments
- Update your address

> ### We've designed
> ### the Harlequin® Reader Service
> ### website just for you.

## Enjoy all the features!

- Reader excerpts from any series
- Respond to mailings and special monthly offers
- Discover new series available to you
- Browse the Bonus Bucks catalog
- Share your feedback

*Visit us at:*

**ReaderService.com**